Praise for The Last Weekend of the Summer:

"Thought provoking, sometimes humorous, sometimes agitating, this is a true slice of life being part of a family of flawed humans."
– Tome Tender

"Will tug on your heart strings!"
– CMash Reads

"A very touching and emotional story!"
– Wall-to-Wall Books

"You're going to need a box of tissues at the end."
– Sunny Island Breezes

"*The Last Weekend of the Summer* is a powerful and compelling story written from the heart. It is a must read that will make you ponder your own family dynamic, stir your soul, and resonate with you for a very long time."
– Jersey Girl Book Reviews

The Last Weekend of the Summer

The Last Weekend of the Summer

Peter Murphy

THE
ST●RY
PLANT

The Story Plant
Studio Digital CT, LLC
P.O. Box 4331
Stamford, CT 06907

Story Plant hardcover ISBN-13: 978-1-61188-257-5
Story Plant paperback ISBN-13: 978-1-61188-271-1
Fiction Studio Books E-book ISBN: 978-1-945839-22-1

Visit our website at www.TheStoryPlant.com

First Story Plant Paperback Printing: October 2019

Printed in the United States of America

0 9 8 7 6 5 4 3 2 1

For my family;
Eduarda,
Damien,
and Aidan.

Chapter 1

Gloria had taken her nap early so she would be well-rested when they all arrived. Sleeping in the afternoon had once seemed such an indulgence, but she knew herself now and how easily she could be worn down. She was eighty-two years old and was grudgingly accepting the growing limitations that came with that.

She sat by the dock and took another hit from her pipe. She smiled her old smile: she would defy her age and get up and spend what energy she could muster with her great-grandchildren. Being with them allowed her to glimpse what it was like to be young again, especially when she was with Susie. She was more like Gloria than all the others. She loved the boys, too: Joey and Dwayne, and little Brad, who always struggled to keep up, but Susie was her favorite.

Gloria exhaled slowly, breathing out some of the little knots that had formed inside of her. Family was the ultimate Gordian knot, and she needed to be in the correct frame of mind.

She had started smoking weed for her glaucoma and was pleasantly surprised by how good it always made her feel. Her doctor had cautioned her about it being a gateway, but as far as Gloria was concerned, there were far bigger problems in the world. She had another few hits and rose to put her pipe away where prying eyes wouldn't find it. Her grandkids, Johnnie, Buddy, and C.C., were okay with her doing it, but their mother, Mary . . . she was another story. And the reason for so many of the knots.

Mary was going to be difficult, and there was very little Gloria would be able to do but try to redirect her for as long as possible. There was a sad predictability about Mary and had been since Jake first brought her home to meet his parents. Gloria had done what she could to make the young woman feel welcome, but Mary had always been rather self-absorbed and very prone to bouts of self-indulgence. And she had never been at ease around Harry on account of his blindness; she often complained to Jake that his father's vacant, empty stare made her feel uncomfortable.

Harry had lost his sight when his bomber was shot up during the war. Thankfully, the pilot had held it together until they made it back across the Channel, saving Harry and what was left of the crew. Still, Harry had to spend almost a year in a hospital in England, and after many months of recuperation back in Canada was deemed fit enough to go out and find his way through the world again.

Like so many of the others who had fought in that war, Harry wanted to seem upbeat and always said that despite losing his sight, and a part of his face, he was one of the luckier ones. He was terribly disfigured, but people didn't concern themselves so much with things like that back then.

Gloria had met him the last time Bert Niosi played the Palais Royale. He had walked right up to her—with the help of her brother—and asked if she could lead. He always enjoyed telling that story, and Gloria had always laughed along with him. She understood: it was one of the ways he reassured himself that he was still able to cope with the world.

After he settled back into civilian life, Harry worked for his father until the old man died, and then Harry took over. He always said that, even blind, he could see far more than his father, and when the time was right, sold the business for a very good price. He sold up their house in North Toronto too and moved Gloria and all her paints and easels into the palatial cottage that had been in his family for years.

Painting was one of the few parts of a much younger Gloria that had survived. Back when she was in her twenties, she had notions of a more bohemian lifestyle: of wearing pants and smoking cigarettes, but convention, and conformity, had shaped her and changed her—at least as far as the world was concerned.

Initially, her parents had mixed feelings about Harry. They were glad that Gloria had found someone, and they were obliged to consider all that he had sacrificed for the common good, but they were concerned that he and Gloria would find it difficult to lead a normal, happy life. Harry and Gloria had scoffed at that and had lived a life full of small eccentricities: small, but enough to reassure them that they would never become like their parents.

The war had changed Harry, and while he always behaved like it hadn't, he was not afraid to share his views with Gloria in private. He said that the war had proven that the people of the world were sheep-like and easily controlled, and that he and Gloria were duty-bound to live to the full extent of the freedoms he, and so many others, had fought for.

That was why he had always supported her painting, and when she had finished a new one, he would touch it as she described all that he could never see. It was a bit odd, but most of life with a blind man was. He was particularly curious as to the colors she had used. That was the one thing he said he missed—colors, particularly at sunset.

When they first got together they had made a vow to never let his sightlessness become an issue, so every fine evening they would sit on the dock and Gloria would describe everything as the light changed. He would smile his odd little smile that was part-wistful and part-defiant. He always said that he savored every moment of it.

For the most part, Gloria had been happy with him, but their last few years were by far the best. They had grown to really know and love each other by then and had learned to ignore the last of each other's shortcomings—the few they hadn't been able to outgrow. The only clouds on their horizon were the ones that blew in from their son's troubled life.

When it was time for Harry to die, he insisted that he would do it on the dock, listening to the soft lap of the lake, the whisperings among the trees, and the lonesome call of the loons. For a few days Gloria had wrapped him in blankets and sat with him as the sun settled just beyond the other shore. They rarely spoke—they didn't have to—and when he drew his last breath, she kissed him and closed his eyes.

Gloria still remembered every detail like it was one of her paintings. She didn't move for a while and just sat holding his hand as it grew colder and colder. Then, when all that he had been was gone, she rose and phoned Jake.

He had reacted poorly and, in the anger of his grief, berated Gloria for not telling him sooner. He would have liked to have known and would have made the trip, if only to say goodbye. Harry hadn't wanted that. Over the previous few years he and Jake had become totally estranged, and Harry wanted to die without any more acrimony—alone with his wife and dancing partner who had led him through the best years of his life. But after he was gone, Gloria grew to understand Jake's rancour and resentment.

She had the chance to make up for that now. She was bringing them all together to try to resolve some old issues while she still could—and it might be just the thing to help Mary find some peace with all that had happened to her along the way.

Gloria smiled to herself as she wrapped her pipe and put it in the old tin box she had kept for years. She placed it beneath the loose board at the shore end of the dock and walked slowly back towards her home.

≈

"Who's dying?"

Johnnie glanced at the rear-view mirror and had to smile. Susie had looked up from her phone and had removed one of her earphones. They'd been crawling along in highway traffic for over an hour and the kids had been off in their electronic bubbles, ignoring everything that was actually said to them but quick to hear what wasn't. He didn't mind; he had decided that they were all going to have a good time, no matter what.

"No one is dying," his wife said over her shoulder. "Are they?" She looked back at Johnnie and waited for him to answer.

He didn't look at her, pretending instead to check his mirrors as if he was going to try to change lanes. There was no point; all three lanes were stop-and-go. It was the last weekend of the summer and everyone was making the most of it, even turning Thursday into Friday. They should have left on Wednesday evening.

"Damn it. I told you that we should have left earlier." He checked the passenger side mirror again and stole a quick glance at Carol. She was smiling. It was how she always looked whenever he thought about her. She was almost forty, but her smile hadn't changed. It was just like when he had finally gotten up the courage to ask her out.

"Well?"

Twenty years later, he still considered it the smartest thing he had ever done—and he'd done a lot of smart things in his life. And Carol had been by his side for most of them.

"Well what? I didn't say anything about anybody dying."

"No, but you did say that it was going to be one last hurrah."

"Yeah," his son joined in, taking a moment to look up from his game.

Johnnie often got frustrated with the amount of time Joey spent playing, but he was doing really well in high school and was, for the most part, a good kid. Carol always reminded Johnnie of that, and that Johnnie was really proud of him—"even if their twisted father/son dynamic didn't allow him to express it verbally." She wasn't serious about the last part; he had a very good and open relationship with his kids. Carol just loved teasing him.

"You only say something like that when someone's about to die."

"I do?"

"Universally, Dad, not everything's about you."

"Well, it should be. I work like a slave, night and day, to put bread on the table for this family. The least I deserve is a bit of recognition once in a while." He tried to keep a straight face but had to turn his head away.

"Really, Johnnie, you're beginning to sound like your mother. I suppose she's riding with Buddy."

"Yeah, and they're probably there by now."

"Good. Maybe she'll have finished complaining by the time we get there."

"Mom, that's not nice," Susie chided absentmindedly as she went back to her phone.

"True, but it's still true. I know she's your grand-mother, but she can be such a . . ."

"And that, kids, is what I mean. I get absolutely no respect." Johnnie checked their faces in the rear-view mirror, but they had their heads down again, tweeting and tagging and toggling. He missed when they were younger and talked about everything they passed along the way. He even missed the choruses of: "Are we there yet?"

They had been coming to the cottage since they were babies. Johnnie was a contractor and helped Gloria keep the place in shape. It was more like a hotel than a cottage, and over the years, Johnnie had restored all the original woodwork and replaced the roofs and the wrap-around veranda. Earlier in the summer he had fitted out the attic of the boathouse and put in bedrooms for the kids. The place was really something.

"So, is she or isn't she?"

"She probably is, but not just yet."

"So, what did you mean by 'one last hurrah'?"

"I just meant it's the end of summer."

Carol nodded and turned back to the windshield. Johnnie did too, towards the long lines of cars that were inching along as far as he could see, each one shimmer-ing in the haze. "Yup! We should have left earlier."

"But you were the one who kept us waiting," Carol teased.

"I had to take that call."

"An emergency renovation?"

"You know we can't let even one get away. It's a dog-eat-dog world out there."

She let it go at that, but he knew that she knew that there was more going on. There was: the call was from his father.

≈

"Text Johnnie and Carol and see where they're at."

Buddy nodded without looking up and began to type with her thumbs, but she kept one eye on Norm. He was getting frustrated, and they'd only just gotten on the highway. She wanted to say that they should have left earlier, but he had a meeting and couldn't get out of it.

Her mother was still miffed at that. She had wanted to get there before Johnnie and Carol, before they had the chance to insinuate themselves with Gloria, who, Mary often complained, made no secret of the fact that they were her favourites. "And," she leaned forward, "you could mention to your brother that I'm not very happy with them right now."

"What did they do now?" Buddy asked dutifully. She wished her mother wouldn't talk like that in front of Norm. It just gave him more things to throw back at her when they argued.

"They never even bothered to ask if I had a ride. For all they care, I could have been left to hitchhike."

"Mom, they knew you were coming with us."

"It wouldn't have killed them to check." Mary sniffed and twitched a little.

"I'll mention it," Buddy nodded again and turned back to her phone.

"And tell him I got a whole box," Norm added after Buddy had been typing for a while.

"A whole box of what?"

"Man things."

"Man things?"

"Cigars. Cubans."

"I hope you're not planning to spend the whole weekend out in the boat."

"Not the whole weekend."

"Norm!"

"Just a few early mornings . . . and a few late nights; I'll be around the rest of the time."

"Napping or just having a few beers?"

"Buddy, come on. Lighten up a bit. After all, the kids are back at school next week."

"All the more reason you should spend as much time with them as you can. I think you should take them with you when you go fishing."

"They're always welcome."

Buddy tried to swallow all the things she really wanted to say. There was no point; when they argued in front of others, she always came away feeling like the bad guy. Everybody—Johnnie, Carol, Gloria—loved Norm. It was easy; he was like a big kid, and she always came off like she was a nag. She turned around to see how the kids were doing, but they didn't look back at her. They were squeezed up against the doors as they tried to avoid making any contact with their grandmother, who always insisted on sitting in the middle and spread out on either side.

"Leave him alone," Mary leaned forward again, squishing them a little more and chiding Buddy like she was still a child. "Let him have a bit of a holiday. He works hard enough—not like your father."

Buddy turned back and stared straight ahead. She knew what her mother was doing. Mary was finding it harder and harder to manage on her own and had talked with Buddy about moving in with her and Norm. She wasn't crazy about the idea, but how could she say no?

Norm had said that he'd need time to think about it and would decide over the weekend. "Let's just have a great weekend, and then we can sit down and talk about it when we get home," he had said, and Buddy knew exactly what he really meant: he was going to hold it over her for as long as he could.

He also said that he had mentioned it to Johnnie and he didn't think it was a good idea. He said that Johnnie felt his mother would be better off in a retirement home. Buddy had gotten a little riled at that, especially when she heard that Carol thought it was time. "It's really not for her to have an opinion on this. This is for Johnnie, C.C., and me to decide."

Even as she had said it, she regretted it, but Norm had just smiled and nodded. She knew exactly what he was thinking. He never argued with her when she went on like that. Later, when it was time to talk about things, he'd often say that he knew she really didn't mean it. And those times when even she had to admit that she had been in the wrong, he'd subtly remind her that just being around her mother always brought out her bitchy side. He'd also suggest that if she had a problem with Carol, she should talk with her about it and not complain through him.

"What did they say?" he asked after Buddy's phone had chirped.

She had it set to some really annoying bird sound that made Mary twitch again. She had explained to them all that she needed it like that to get her attention because she was so always busy most of the time. She had a point. Norm had to work late a lot recently, and she had to take the kids to all their stuff. She just needed some time to chill and, with her mother around, that wasn't going to happen so much. For Buddy, being at the cottage wasn't a time for relaxing. She had to deal with the kids—and her mother—without all the conveniences and distractions of home. Norm just didn't seem to get that.

"They're just coming up to Orillia."

"Hey, we can catch them." Norm changed lanes for the umpteenth time. He got a few cars ahead before the whole highway ground to a halt again. "We should have left earlier. Damn it."

≈

"Do you want to stop somewhere and let them catch up?" Johnnie asked. He had his elbow out the open window. It was his James Dean pose, and it still made Carol feel good inside. They had really gotten into all that fifties stuff after they had seen *Grease* one night at a drive-in, and Johnnie still rented a convertible for their anniversaries and stuff, but it looked just as cool when he did it in the truck.

"What do you want to do?"

She hoped he wouldn't. She was fine with Norm and Buddy. She just wasn't ready to face her mother-in-law yet. She almost wished she wasn't coming. Mary never handled these weekends well and would spend the first day winding everybody up, picking on her children about how they were raising their children. And then, when everybody was just about to start plotting how they'd like to kill her and dump her body in the lake, she'd pull out all the terrible things life had done to her with a special emphasis on Johnnie's father starring role.

Weekends at the cottage were a very mixed bag. The kids got to have a blast. And Johnnie got to unwind—after he had done whatever needed fixing, but sometimes being around his family took so much effort. Carol loved Gloria, and Buddy, even though she sometimes made it so hard. Norm too; he was such a loveable clown. Even C.C. was okay. Carol had known her since she was a kid, and that helped. Mary was another story, and when they were all together—it was like they stopped being who they really were and all became characters in some drawn-out soap opera.

"I wouldn't mind stopping at a Tim's," Johnnie announced, languidly—the way he did when he didn't really care one way or the other. "But we don't have to tell them if you don't want."

"You know it's not them, right?" It was Mary and how she could get them all dancing on the end of her strings.

"I know, but we got to talk them out of this. We can't let them do this to each other."

"I don't think we can stop them." She wanted to leave it at that—at least for now. She never shared her true feelings about Mary with Johnnie—at least not directly. Mary was his mother; there was no point. Besides, they had been together long enough to know exactly what the other was thinking. Besides, it was family. What could you do?

"We got to try."

"Is Granny going to live with Aunt Buddy?" Susie asked from the back seat, and even Joey looked up.

"No," Carol said with a straight face. "She's coming to live with us, and we're going to give her your room."

"I'm serious." Susie shoved her brother, who was laughing even as he clicked away. "It's just she makes everything so . . ."

"Don't worry," Carol turned around and smiled at her daughter. "We'll put her in your brother's room."

"Ask them if they've heard from C.C.," Johnnie asked after winking at his son through the rear-view mirror. "I left messages for her, but I haven't heard back."

"You know your little sister," Carol laughed as she began to text. "She'll want to make her usual grand entrance."

≈

Norm looked over when Buddy's phone chirped again.

"They're asking when C.C.'s coming," Buddy offered as she texted back.

"And?"

"Friday morning."

Norm didn't turn as his wife watched and waited for his reaction. She had this thing stuck in her mind about him and her little sister. C.C. was seven years younger than Buddy and, for the last few years, had come for weekends at the cottage with a series of love-struck men on her arm. She had always been so flippant and casual with them, and that just seemed to make them want her all the more. Norm always said that she was a tease, but Johnnie and Carol always ribbed him about being just as attentive. That used to bother Buddy, but two years ago, C.C. created a flutter when she turned up with a beautiful woman named Michelle, especially with their mother, who insisted that she was just concerned about what Gloria might think.

Gloria had just laughed about it and said that it all made sense to her now. She also thought Michelle didn't seem the type that would fawn over C.C.

Between Christmases, Thanksgivings, and other weekends, Michelle quickly became a part of the family until she and C.C. broke up in the spring. It was the first time C.C. had ever been dumped, and they all couldn't help but feel a little sorry for her. But C.C. seemed to have bounced back and had called to let them know that she was bringing her new partner with her.

Still, despite all of C.C.'s bluster and bravado, Buddy claimed that she could see right through her. C.C., she had confided in them all, was lost and confused, and despite all of her kidding around, was just trying to deflect from the fact that deep down inside she probably wished she could be more like Buddy, settled and with kids.

She said it was because their parents' break-up had been very hard on them all, but particularly hard on C.C. She was only five at the time and couldn't understand. Their mother had been no help at all, constantly breaking down and crying about all the terrible things their father had done—and what a terrible human being he was. It was no wonder C.C. had grown up with so many issues. Buddy and Johnnie had done all they could, but they were just kids too. Sometimes, Buddy felt so angry towards her mother, but she could never say anything. Her mother was fragile at the best of times.

Buddy knew that C.C. was fragile too, no matter how much she pretended she was all tough and hip, and Buddy always had to keep an eye on her along with everything else she had to do. But at least she'd been able to get their mother to accept C.C.'s life choices. Buddy and Johnnie had learned to live with their mother's constant censure: C.C. hadn't, and she had classic daddy issues.

Everybody had been fine with the news of C.C.'s new partner—even her mother, who just sniffed a little. "Well, as long as she is happy this time."

Hopefully all would go well. C.C. had a tendency to fly off the handle if anyone even thought about reproaching her about how she chose to lead her life. Even their mother was hesitant to criticize her openly and preferred to channel her disapproval through Buddy. Usually beginning with: "Someone should really have a talk with her about..."

≈

"I just wish you had given me a bit more notice."

Heather seemed mildly annoyed, so C.C. gave her the smile—the one that always got her out of trouble. "I did tell you not to make plans for the weekend."

"Yes, but you never said we were going to spend it with your entire family."

Heather was nervous. She fidgeted with her bangs, and her bright blue eyes were even bigger. She was as blond as Michelle had been dark. C.C. was her first, apart from some heavy petting when she was away at college. They had met at a party and Heather had been a little drunk. The following morning, she was full of doubt, but C.C. had told her it was normal—that all virgins went through that.

"Well, consider this a dry run."

"But we're going to be there for whole weekend. What if they don't like me?"

C.C. probably should have given her more notice, but she didn't want to risk giving her a chance to back out. She couldn't bear the idea of showing up alone. She needed them to know that she had moved on from Michelle. And she didn't want any of them to feel sorry for her. "Don't worry. They'll love you. My mother can be a total pain sometimes, but my brother and sister are cool."

"Who else is going to be there?"

"My brother's wife and kids—you'll like them—and my sister's husband and their kids. He can be a bit too much at times."

"What do you mean?"

"He gets a bit too friendly."

"Even..."

"More so, but you'll love my gran. She tokes up, only no one is supposed to notice. My mother will be there too, but we all try to ignore her."

"Great: The whole family."

"Well, yeah, except my father. He and my mother have been divorced for more than twenty-five years. The rest of us hang out fairly often, but this weekend is going to be a little different. I think my grandmother might be dying."

"Oh my God, I'm so sorry, C.C."

"Yeah," C.C. agreed, sensing Heather's reticence fade. She smiled as innocently as she could and reached across the table to hold her hand. "That's why I need you there with me."

Chapter 2

As the truck slithered to a halt on the gravel road, Susie and Joey took off. It was one of their cottage rituals, running to Gloria who stood waving from the veranda. For the last few years, Joey had let Susie win but had always made it look like he was running as fast as he could. Johnnie and Carol sat back and watched. They always gave the kids a few moments with Gloria before they joined them.

"So, what's really going on?" Carol asked without looking over at him.

"What do you mean?"

"There's a little dark cloud hovering over your head."

"Damn. I was hoping you wouldn't notice it."

"Come on, out with it."

"Dad's coming too. He's coming sometime Saturday morning."

"Does your mother know?"

"I don't think so. Gloria wanted to break the news to everyone at the same time."

"Oh dear, so Buddy doesn't know yet?"

"No, and there's more."

There always was with his family, but Carol didn't say that. Instead, she just sat for a moment taking it all in. And when he was finished, she squeezed his hand

and leaned across to kiss his cheek. "I'm so sorry to hear that. Are you going to be okay?"

"Don't worry about me; I'll be fine. And we're all going to have a great time, no matter what." He smiled and winked at her. "Ready?"

"Showtime," she smiled back, and she got out and walked towards the veranda. She knew what he was doing; he was getting himself ready for another weekend of enabling his sisters and his mother. She wished he wouldn't, but there was no point in saying that. Instead, she'd be as loving and supportive as he needed her to be. It was how they dealt with life—along with having a laugh at themselves. "And stop checking out my ass," she called over her shoulder as she went.

"Better yours than someone else's," Gloria laughed as she slowly descended the stairs from the veranda and kissed Carol's cheek. She still had the most remarkable hearing. "That was something my Harry always used to say."

"Really, Gloria, I wouldn't have thought stuff like that would have been a problem for you guys."

"He was blind, Carol, but he was still a man."

Carol pretended to look shocked, but Gloria carried on as if she didn't notice. "But you have nothing to worry about. Johnnie's still madly in love with you, isn't he, dear?" Gloria had a twinkle in her eye.

"Of course he is. And I'm still crazy about him—just don't tell him."

"I hope so, dear, because I put you two in the east room. I know it's your favorite."

"Thanks," Carol took the old, brittle woman into her arms. "And are you okay, Gloria?"

"Of course I am. Why would you ask such a thing?" But she stayed in Carol's arms for a little while longer.

"What are you two plotting?" Johnnie asked as he struggled up with their bags. "And don't worry about me—I'll just lug everybody's stuff by myself."

"And, well, you should," Gloria reached up and kissed him, and hugged him as tight as her frail old arms would allow. "Your poor wife and children are here for a rest, so don't be selfish and go around spoiling everything.

"So," Gloria asked after Carol had gone to settle the kids into the new rooms over the boathouse. "Have you talked with your father?" She waited at the bottom step for Johnnie to take her by the elbow. She could have made it on her own, but she knew he liked to behave like a gentleman.

"Yes, and I hope he knows what he's doing. It might be asking a bit too much."

"Not of you, dear, surely?"

"No, I'm okay with it all, and I really want this to work out—for everyone. I was a bit torn up when I first heard, but it's settled in now and, well, you know . . ."

"Yes, Johnnie, I do." She smiled up at him and reached up to stroke his cheek. It always reminded her of Harry's—at least his good side. "Being family means having to go through things like this, and we will all get to play our parts. Hopefully C.C.'s new love interest will provide enough distraction for your mother."

She paused when they got to the top step and looked up at him for a moment as if she was about to say something else but changed her mind.

"What is it, Gloria? What other secrets are you keeping from me?"

"Far too many for what little time we have left. Now let's go inside. I have some nice cold beer in the fridge. You might need some fortification before your mother gets here."

≈

The others arrived almost two and a half hours later, and Buddy was clearly frustrated. Mary had insisted on stopping to pick up more groceries even though Johnnie and Carol had told them they had already looked after it.

Mary however, seemed almost content and, as they turned off the main road, announced that she was ready to take charge and make sure that her grandchildren did not wear Gloria out.

Gloria, she had told them, almost confidentially as she leaned forward into the space between the front seats, could be very self-indulgent that way. She would insist on trying to keep up with the kids until she was exhausted. Then it would fall to Mary to make sure she got some rest. The others didn't seem to understand that. They were more than happy to just dump their kids for a few hours. Mary would have to step in.

Not so much with their children, she assured Norm and Buddy. It was more Johnnie's two. They were more like their mother—especially Susie, who could get a bit sassy every now and then. It would be a bit of a challenge, Mary sighed as she sat back between her grandchildren, but she didn't mind. She just wanted to make sure that everybody had a chance to relax and enjoy themselves.

Her words lingered as the car crunched the gravel and came to a stop.

"Norm?" Buddy called over to him after they had gotten out, and he stood looking towards the dock where Johnnie and Carol were sitting. "You are going to help us unpack?"

He stood with his box of cigars in one hand and a case of beer in the other like he had been caught doing something he shouldn't do. "Sure. Let me drop these off first."

"Let him have a few minutes," Mary answered before Buddy could react. "He's been driving in traffic all day. Let him go, and you and I will see to what needs doing."

Norm smiled his most innocent smile, and Buddy let it go at that. She would deal with him later, when they were alone. "Dwayne, Brad—please take your sleeping bags with you."

"But we want to see Granny Gloria."

"Let them go," Mary intruded again. "You and I can manage here."

"Wait, let me help," Carol called out as she made her way over from the dock.

"That's so kind of you," Mary thanked her without making eye contact. "But there is no need. Buddy and I have everything under control."

"We do?" Buddy tried to sound amused. "Take those first," she nodded to Carol. "They should be put in the fridge as soon as possible."

"Did you clear out an entire Loblaws?" Carol looked bemused as they unpacked so many things that she and Johnnie had already brought.

"Tell me about it," Buddy muttered so her mother wouldn't hear. She was wound tight and went on unpacking, mechanically pulling bags from the back of the car and handing them to Mary or Carol depending on their weight.

"Here," Carol offered when they had finally finished and settled around the kitchen table. "Have a glass of wine."

"It's too early for red wine."

"Not at the cottage. Besides, the white is not cold."

"Okay, then. Hit me."

"Mary?"

"Oh no, dear, it's far too early for me, but you two go ahead. I'll just go over to the boathouse and check on the children. We don't want them wearing poor Gloria out on the first day."

She seemed very content with that and walked away.

"Should we go with her?"

"Nay, Gloria can handle her."

≈

By late afternoon it was sultry, and the kids were cooling off in the lake, swimming around the dock where Gloria sat. Johnnie had roped off an area, and the kids had to stay within that. Even Joey, who was strong enough to swim out to the island and back, had agreed but was diving off the deeper end.

Susie stayed closer to the shore and kept an eye on the younger kids, particularly Brad, who was still using water wings. Susie was very patient with him and deflected the ribbing from his brother. Brad could manage fine without them, but Buddy had insisted and Gloria had suggested that they all go along with it for now.

It usually took Buddy a day to unwind and relax, particularly when it came to her children. Gloria had often tried to talk with her about that, but Buddy took after Mary that way, and it never did any good to point that out. Instead, Gloria sat and fanned herself. It was getting too hot for her—and her buzz was wearing off.

"Are you okay, Gigi?" Susie asked and hauled herself up on the dock, the water streaming off her long, tanned body. She was starting to become a woman, but at times she still looked more like a foal, especially when she folded her long legs beneath her.

"Yes. Don't worry about me. I have been sitting here, summers and winters, since long before you were born. Besides, you're not here to worry about an old woman like me."

"I'm not worried, Gigi. I was just asking because your face looks tired."

"That's because I spent most of my life smiling."

"I hope I can say things like that when I get old."

"I hope so too because you have the most beautiful smile. Sometimes, when you're all back in the city, I think about your smile and it makes me feel warm." She had also painted it and was going to give it to Susie at the end of the weekend. She just had to find a time when nobody would notice. She didn't want it to set anything off.

"My dad says I got it from you."

"Well, maybe that's why I like it so much."

Susie rose and kissed her great-grandmother's brow and then plunged back into the water, showering them all with the spray. Gloria didn't mind; the laughter of her great-grandchildren was the perfect fall song for her life.

She turned as someone approached and watched Mary make her way towards her. She was far too heavy, and even the short walk from the cottage was taking a toll on her. She had put on the weight years ago when she and Jake had split, and despite her constant complaints and grumblings about her health, could never seem to bring herself to do anything about it. Gloria had given up trying to talk to her about things like that. Mary had chosen to be a victim, and until she was ready to change, there was nothing anyone else could do.

"Gloria, shouldn't you be sitting in the shade?"

≈

"I don't care. I want to leave."

Mary had come back from the dock and was almost hysterical.

"Mother," Buddy walked towards her with her arms wide. "Please?"

"Did you know?" Mary asked and stood back, looking horrified. Gloria had told her that Jake was coming, and Mary had reacted predictably.

"No, mother, I didn't. No one bothered to mention it to me, either." Buddy shot a quick glance of disapproval at Johnnie and Carol who both looked away. They should have discussed it with her. She might have been able to break the news to Mary in a way that could have avoided such a scene.

"Well, if any of you think," Mary continued to no one in particular, "that I'm going to spend the weekend in the same house as that man after all he did to me..." She shuddered and cried a little before looking up. "How can you all be so cruel?"

Susie and the rest of the kids had come back from the lake and were standing near the door, unsure as to what to do next. Brad had tried to go to his mother, but Joey held on to him while Susie tried to distract Dwayne. "Perhaps," Carol walked towards them, "you guys could start gathering sticks for the fire tonight? Grandma's not feeling well and should lie down."

"Yes," Buddy agreed and stepped in front of Carol. "We will have a prize for who gathers the most."

Joey shot a quick glance at his father who nodded. Joey nodded back, and he took his two cousins by the shoulders and turned them towards the door, but Susie lingered until Gloria nodded to her.

"Mary, dear," she continued when the kids were gone. "I didn't mention it earlier because I thought it would be better to tell you face-to-face. I knew you'd be upset."

"Well, I am, and I want to leave. If I had known what you were all plotting ... well, I certainly wouldn't have come. Don't any of you remember the things that man put me through?"

She heaved like she was pulling her umbrage up from her own depths. "No! I cannot be part of this. I'm sorry, but my nerves would not be able for it." She paused to release all the shuddering and gasping she had done. "Will one of you please drive me?" She looked around and caught Norm's eye before he could turn away. "Please?"

"Perhaps," Carol intruded to save Norm's blushes, "you might want to lie down for a little while. I'm sure this has come as a bit of a shock, but after you lie down we can talk about it and, if you still want to leave, Johnnie and I will drive you back."

"Or Norm and I will." Buddy interjected and walked over to take her mother's arm. "But Carol is right; you should lie down first—to get over the shock."

≈

"Why is he coming?" Norm asked after Buddy had taken Mary to her room and Gloria had gone to check on the kids. Carol had offered to do it, but Gloria had insisted.

Johnnie waited until they had gone far enough before he answered. "Because of Gloria." He checked Norm's face for his reactions and softly added, "It might be the last chance we all have to spend a weekend together."

"Shit." Norm shook his head before looking across at Johnnie and Carol. "Why didn't you guys tell us?"

"We wanted to, but Gloria insisted it would better coming from her first." Johnnie looked at Norm as knowingly as he could. Carol always said that it made him look confused, but Norm usually bought it. But this time, he wasn't really listening. He was probably trying to find a way to say that they could have handled it, but they all knew that

Buddy would have panicked and told Mary, and she would have dug in her heels, or something. Not that finding out the way she did was going to make it any easier.

"Does C.C. know?" Norm finally asked.

"I don't think so, unless Gloria told her."

"Shit! I'm going to miss the old girl."

"C'mon," Johnnie offered to change the mood and, after a sidelong glance at Carol, rose and headed toward the fridge. "Let's grab a couple of brewskis and go see what vandalism the kids have gotten up to. And bring two of those cigars you've been going on about. We might need to stay outside for a while."

"Don't forget," Carol smiled at them, extra sweetly to make her point. "You two are on barbeque duty tonight."

"Peck, peck, peck. Do you ever give it a rest?"

"That's exactly what Buddy and I are planning to do. We're going to sit by the dock and watch the lake for a while. Please keep the kids busy so we can have some time alone."

"But what about us? When do we get to have some boys' time?" Norm tried to make it sound like he was serious, but Johnnie was already heading for the door.

"Right now," Carol assured him as she struggled to keep from smiling. "You can take the kids into the woods and teach them how to do man stuff."

"Man stuff?"

"Yeah, like knowing when to give your hard-working wife some R&R."

"Yeah," Gloria chimed in from the doorway. "The women of the tribe need to hold a council. You and Johnnie should take the kids off and hunt and gather things."

Norm stood, not knowing what to say when Johnnie called to him, "You gotta learn to know when you're beat, dude."

"Gloria and I are going to go down to the dock. Coming?" Carol asked as Buddy came down the stairs.

"But what about Mom?"

"Oh, she'll be fine." Gloria rose and took her grand-daughter by the arm, linking Carol with the other. "Mary just needs a little time to sulk. She's always been like that. She'll come down when she's good and ready, and I'm sure she'll see to it that we all pay for our transgres-sions then. Let's go and prepare ourselves. It's going to be a very long weekend.

≈

"And you still think this was a good idea?" Carol asked after they had sat for a while in silence, listening to the lap of the lake water and the rustle of the trees. Gloria looked a little less sure of herself, and Buddy seemed to be lost inside of her own head. She never said much about her feelings toward her father, and even though she always sided with her mother when the subject was raised, she had always seemed conflicted.

"It is the way it should be." Gloria nodded and looked at each of them in turn. She paused until they both looked back. "We will all need closure." She almost seemed to tremble as her words lingered in the warm air. "Perhaps it is a little selfish of me, but I wanted you all here with me this weekend. I wanted my entire family to be together once more, while there is still time."

Buddy said nothing and looked so sad that Carol had to reach over and put her arm around her. They were sitting like kids at Gloria's feet, with their own feet dan-gling off the edge of the dock. "I guess that is as good a reason as any. Eh, Buddy?"

But Buddy didn't answer; she was staring off across the surface of the lake to where the settling sun caught on every wrinkle the warm breeze made.

"Rosemary?" Gloria asked and reached out to touch her granddaughter's hair. "Rosebud?"

"What? Sorry, I was miles away."

"Are you going to be okay?"

"Don't worry about me, Gloria; I'll be fine. It's my mother I'm worried about."

"Dear, this might be the opportunity your mother needs to come to terms with the past."

"Yeah, no. I'm not even sure that I can."

"Of course you can, Rosebud. One of the advantages of becoming an old woman is that I have realized that while the past may be full of errors, the present is full of opportunities to make amends."

"Perhaps, but I am not sure that my mother has arrived at the point where she might agree."

"Then, my dears, let us make it our job to help her get there."

Carol nodded in agreement, but Buddy seemed less sure. "Easier said than done," she muttered.

Gloria looked at her and waited for a moment. "But we will try. When Mary gets up, let's all behave like it's no big deal. Let's all just carry on like it's a normal weekend and the whole family is just here to celebrate the end of summer. Trust me, it will be better for Mary when she realizes that no one is going to pay any mind to her tantrums."

"Gigi?" Susie called out loudly from the path so they would know she was coming.

"Yes, dear." Gloria answered and forced herself to smile.

"Daddy and Uncle Norm are ready to start barbequing."

"And they need us there because?" Carol answered and rose to meet her daughter, giving her the biggest hug when she got there.

≈

Mary was more than a little taciturn when they all sat down to eat, but everyone tried to carry on regardless. Carol and Buddy were trying so hard that Gloria chided them a few times and told them they were drinking their wine too fast, and that just made the two of them laugh even more.

"Looks like we've got some catching up to do," Norm said knowingly and reached into the cooler for two more beers.

"Not for me, bro," Johnnie declined. "I'm going to take the kids out on the boat after we eat."

"But you've only had two."

"Don't worry. I'll catch up later."

"Can Buddy and I come on your boat?" Carol asked and pointed her half-eaten hotdog at her husband. "A nice cruise on the lake would really set the mood. Eh, Buddy?"

"Sorry, kids only."

"But we're still kids at heart," Buddy joined in causing the two of them to start to giggle.

"Maybe," Norm winked at Johnnie, "the four of us could go out in the canoes later."

"Ooh," Buddy and Carol cooed together.

"What's got into those two?" Mary asked no one in particular.

"Oh, let them enjoy themselves," Gloria said before anyone else could. "You and I can sit on the veranda and listen to the crickets."

"And who will look after the children?"

"We will," Joey and Susie said, almost in unison. Johnnie had put a DVD player in their room in the boathouse. They could watch scary movies after the little ones had fallen asleep. Johnnie had even let Joey smuggle two beers over.

"Children minding children," Mary sniffed and twitched a little. "I don't think it is right."

"We're all somebody's children." Gloria looked at each one in turn, smiling her old crinkled smile. "And I love every one of you."

"And we all love you," Susie agreed from behind her ear of corn. Johnnie had seared the tips of the kernels, just the way she liked it.

"But I love you the most," Brad piped up. His mouth was smeared with ketchup and mustard. He looked around until they all laughed.

"Do not," Dwayne nudged his way into the spotlight.

"Do so."

"Do not."

"Well, I love Granny Gigi the mostest," Norm almost burped as he swigged from his beer.

"Really, Norm?" Buddy tried to keep a straight face but began to giggle again.

≈

After the kids had helped Johnnie and Norm clear everything away, and everyone had gone off to enjoy the warm evening, Gloria sat with Mary on the old swing seat on the veranda. Carol had made them a jug of iced tea with a little something added. Mary had been reticent at first, but Gloria knew how to coax her past that, at least for now. It would be another story when Jake arrived, but Gloria had learned to take life one day at a time. "Everything will be fine in the end. You'll see."

"You're not the one he betrayed."

Gloria turned so she could look straight into her daughter-in-law's eyes. "Mary, dear, isn't it time you faced the truth about what really happened? At least admit it to yourself."

Chapter 3

On Friday morning, Johnnie woke at five thirty, just as he had planned. He didn't have to set the alarm. Life with his family had taught him to become self-reliant—even before his parents separated. He was in his mid-teens then, but from the beginning their constant bickering and endless games of emotional tug-of-war had left him feeling that he had to look after himself—and his little sisters. He took pride in that. Sometimes Carol teased him about it, but other times she admitted that it was one of a great many things she loved about him.

She was draped across him, but he managed to slide out of the bed without waking her. She could sleep through anything when she was content—and she was. When they had finally gotten to bed, they had taken the time to make love. She still did it for him. The longer they were together, the better it became. He knew every curve of her body by now, and he knew where and how she liked to be touched. She was the same with him.

He had left his clothes where he could easily find them and dressed in the dark. He opened the door and stepped out into the hall as Norm emerged from his room. Buddy muttered something from the bed behind him, and Norm whispered something back before he turned and winked at Johnnie. "C'mon then, let's get at them."

The old stairs creaked and groaned a few times as they went down. They were hoping not to disturb the others, but the light was on in the kitchen and there was a delicious smell of peameal.

"I made a flask of coffee and sandwiches for you to take out with you." Gloria stood in the middle of her kitchen, looking tired but happy. A few strands of her grey hair had strayed across her forehead, and her hands were white and wrinkled.

"Gloria, you didn't have to."

"Well, as a matter of fact, I did. I have a favor to ask: I need you to take a look at the septic tank, later."

"I can do it now," Johnnie offered, to Norm's consternation.

"No. It can wait until you have caught some fish. The man from the town was supposed to come by this week, but he hasn't." She wasn't complaining; she just said it as a matter of fact. "Besides, I need you boys to catch some nice trout. I haven't had trout for breakfast since the spring."

"Sure," Norm agreed and took the wrapped sandwiches. "What size and how many?"

"More than you normally manage, dear," Gloria answered with a straight face.

"You just got burned, bro." Johnnie laughed and gave the old woman a hug. "Still got it, eh Gloria?"

"Careful, bro," Norm warned as they headed for the door. "Or you just might end up having to stir the shit on your own."

After they had finally loaded everything and rearranged it a few times for balance, they paddled out beyond the island and let the canoe drift along among the reflected clouds. The sky was getting brighter and the lake was almost still except for the little ripples where fish poked through to catch flies. Smaller fry leapt clear out of the water, but even those splashes quickly subsided, and the surface grew calm as coral and mirrored the pearled skies. But beneath, where the light began to fade among reeds and rushes, everything was hungry, and it wasn't long before they both had a few bites.

"Now, this is the life," Norm laughed as he finished the last of the sandwiches. Gloria had made them two each, and she hadn't been stingy with the bacon. "It almost makes all the rest of the shit worthwhile." He had added some whiskey to the coffee too and was brimming over with the joys of living.

"Not to break the mood, or anything," Johnnie said offhandedly as he flicked his rod and deftly hooked another. His reel clicked softly as he calmly hauled it towards him. "But are you and Buddy really going to go through with it?"

"What choice do I have?"

"Listen, bro. She's my mother, and I know what she can be like."

"I know, but Buddy seems set on it."

"She's just feeling guilty. You got to sit down and have a talk with her."

"I dunno, man. It might be better just to let things sort themselves out."

"Maybe, but I know my mother, Norm. She will make both of your lives a misery."

"It will be anyway—if I don't." He paused to check on Johnnie's reaction. He loved his sister, and his mother, but Norm knew he could talk to him about stuff like that—stuff he really couldn't say to anybody else.

"You need to talk with Buddy, man. You guys can't do this to yourselves."

"Yeah, but you know what she gets like. Hey, maybe you could try talking to her?"

"Hell no, man. I got more than enough family stuff to deal with. Just talk with your wife and tell her how you really feel about having your mother-in-law come live with you."

"Do you think she'll understand?"

"No way, but at least when the shit hits the fan, you can say you were against it all along."

"And what good will that do?"

Johnnie had wanted to make him laugh, but Norm wasn't up for it. "Not much, but at least you will have said something. You can't just let it happen."

"Yeah, except you know what she can be like." Norm shook his head and jerked his rod, missing another bite. He really didn't have the patience for fishing. He just liked being out with Johnnie. "I don't suppose that you could just tell her that we need to talk?"

"I'll think about it."

"Thanks, man. Only don't let her know that we talked about it."

≈

"Wow. You guys actually caught something."

Buddy and Carol were sitting and drinking coffee on the veranda with Gloria, who had tried to convince them of the benefits of her own selection of herbal teas. It looked too much like roadside weeds and scraggly flowers, so they both declined, much to Gloria's chagrin.

"Of course they did," Gloria chided them with just a hint of rancour. "Men are still very capable—in their own milieu. I know it's very fashionable these days to make all men out as oafs, but it's just a reflection of how today's women have become mean-spirited."

"Wow," Carol mouthed at Buddy to deflect the sting.

"Things were much better when we treated men with a little respect. And we didn't go around talking about our vaginas all the time."

"I certainly don't go around talking about things like that." Buddy was getting a little defensive. "Do I, Carol?"

"Not you, dear," Gloria corrected her. "I am talking about modern culture—like on the TV. Every night I sit and watch ads were the men are all useless boobs and the women are obsessed with their personal hygiene."

"Please, Gloria," Carol interjected. "We're about to have breakfast."

"Provided by the hunters of the tribe," Norm reminded them as he sat beside his wife and smiled.

"Go on, then," Gloria prodded Buddy. "Say something nice to him."

"Very well," Buddy sipped her coffee and forced a smile. "Thank you, love of my life, for getting up early and braving the elements to catch all these fish for us and our children."

"Maybe, the next time," Gloria patted Buddy's shoulder. "You could try with less sarcasm. Now, your turn," Gloria turned to Carol. "Don't you have anything to say to your husband—especially after last night?"

"Gloria, were you listening?"

"Not deliberately, but you have always been a loud and enthusiastic lover, dear."

"What?" Carol almost stammered and blushed a little. "Really, Gloria?"

"Oh, don't pretend to be prissy with me, young miss. We've all known each other long enough to be honest once in a while. Now give me the fish, and I will get them ready."

"No," Johnnie protested, but Gloria wouldn't hear any of it.

"Joey and Susie have agreed to help."

"At least let me clean them."

"Not at all; I gave Joey your grandfather's knife, and he can't wait to use it."

"Wow," Buddy laughed after she had gone inside. "Gloria's on fire this morning."

"Yeah," Johnnie shook his head and laughed. "Only, I'm not sure about Joey and the knife. It's a Bowie. Carol? Carol, don't you have anything to say about our angst-ridden delinquent getting a knife?"

"She called me 'young miss.' Go away and let me enjoy it for a while."

"Morning," Susie interrupted them all as she emerged with a tray of coffee cups and glasses of orange juice with champagne. "Courtesy of Gigi. She also said you're all to sit here while we make breakfast."

They all thanked her, except Carol who just smiled up at her. "She called me 'young miss.'"

≈

"Is Mary not joining us?"

"No," Gloria said as her lips pursed a little. "She has decided to take her breakfast by the dock."

"Is she over there alone?"

"Of course not, dear; I sent Dwayne and Brad over to keep her company. If she wants to behave like a child, then let her sit at the kiddie's table. And now let's eat."

Buddy might have reacted, but Joey and Susie brought out the fish, fried in butter and covered with wild mushrooms, and took their places at the adult's table; Gloria had decided it was time. "And where are you off to?" she asked as Buddy tried to rise.

"I was just going over to check on the kids."

"They'll be fine. I told them that if they were good and looked after Mary, they could have s'mores tonight—as many as they want. Now, please eat and relax. Just enjoy the peace while it lasts."

≈

Afterwards, when all the fish were eaten and everything had been cleared away, Buddy had to go to check on her mother. She was sitting stiffly, and when she spoke to her grandchildren, her voice was strained. She was obviously still upset, sniffling and twitching her head. It was a sure sign that trouble was brewing. Buddy knew she would regret it, but she had to ask.

"Everything okay, Mom?"

"I'm fine, dear, all things considered. I'm just worried about Gloria."

Buddy knew she should try to deflect her, but she also knew that she couldn't. After the shock she'd had, her mother needed to vent a little.

"I know she is just being brave, but she will just wear herself down, and then I'm the one that has to worry about her."

"But we're all here, Mom."

"I knew you are, dear, but I don't think we should expect too much help from her." She rolled her eyes in the direction of the lake where Carol was skiing. She was wearing her yellow bikini, and against her bronzed skin it made her look . . . well, nothing like a mother of teenagers should look. Buddy had brought her bikini too, but she wasn't ready to wear it. Her black one-piece was far more forgiving.

"Look at her. She shouldn't be going around like that in front of her children. It will just confuse them.

And that boy of hers is far too young to be handling that boat."

"Well, I think she looks great."

"That's because you're being kind, dear. You take after me in that. I never have a bad word to say about anybody—unless they deserve it.

"Oh, my God," Mary added after she had turned to look out at the lake again. "Tell her to stop before my nerves are frayed away." Carol was goofing around, holding on with one hand and stepping over to hold the grip backwards. "What kind of example is that to be giving her daughter?"

Buddy couldn't help but smile. Even as she approached forty, Carol still had her gymnastic skills. She'd even been a cheerleader in high school, except she wasn't like the cheerleaders at Buddy's school. Carol was the closest thing she had to a real friend, and not even her mother's insinuations could crowd that out. "Well, I think she should be out enjoying herself. She works hard enough."

"What work? All she does is talk on the phone all day."

Carol did much more than that. She ran the business side of things and let Johnnie do what he loved most— work with his hands.

"Well, I'm going to join them. Perhaps you should have a little nap before C.C. gets here. Gloria is already lying down."

"How can I rest knowing that shit-face will be here tomorrow?"

"Mother, I hope you are not going to call him that in front of the kids."

"Why not? They should know what he is really like."

"Mother, Gloria wants us to do this. Let's just make the best of it. For her sake."

"Everybody is much more concerned about her, and nobody stops to consider what this might be doing to me."

"We do, Mom. We appreciate everything you have ever done—for all of us. And right now, we need you to set a good example—for all of us. It will be something the kids will remember when they are grown and have problems of their own."

"Well, you know me; I would do anything for my grandchildren."

≈

"How come you and I always get to clean up this family's shit?"

Norm and Johnnie had done what had to be done and were heading back to shower and crack open a few beers.

"It's a man's life, bro. We spend most of our lives putting bread on the table—and the rest wiping up afterwards."

"Right, like you're struggling. I've seen what you charge for slapping cheap paint over your rickety work. I'm the one who has to grind out every nickel."

"Suck it up, bro. It's going to be worse when my mother moves in with you."

"Don't remind me. Hey, how do you think it's going to go down when your old man gets here?"

"I have no idea, but Gloria says she has it covered."

"Really?"

"That's what she says, but I'm still expecting the worst."

"Yeah, Buddy's pretty mixed up about it too. She says it's because of her mother, but I don't buy that."

"Yeah, there's nothing like being back with your parents to bring out the kid in everyone again."

"Your mother isn't saying too much."

"Yeah, Gloria must have said something to her."

"Isn't that a good thing?"

"Boy, do you have a lot to learn. But look on the bright side; you get to check out C.C.'s new girlfriend."

"Yeah. Hey, wait a minute. Are you saying . . .?"

"No. I'm not saying anything. Just don't let Buddy catch you this time."

≈

When they got to the edge of the road, C.C. shut off the car, and she and Heather sat for a while, staring at the windshield in silence. For the last hour or so, their efforts at conversation had become more and more stilted. C.C. had stopped trying to reassure Heather and had gotten lost in her own thoughts, cranking up the A/C and the music to fill the car with noise.

"Well, we're here," she finally broke the silence. "C'mon, everyone must be down by the lake. And don't worry," she added as Heather hesitated. "They're going to love you." C.C. smiled for emphasis, but it was a little strained. Her mind was elsewhere.

"How can you be so sure?" Heather asked and checked herself in the visor mirror.

"Because you're so adorable."

C.C. leaned across to kiss her, but Heather recoiled a little. "What if someone sees?"

"Then they would know if we loved each other— or not." She leaned back and smiled. She waited until Heater looked into her eyes and then turned away and got out.

Heather followed across the grass—like a cat, ready at any moment to dash.

"We're here," C.C. called out, but the warm, heavy air made her voice sound muffled.

"We're here," C.C. called again, hoping someone would answer to break the tension.

She turned to smile at Heather, but she had her head down as she picked her way through the grass. She had worn her new sandals, and while they made her feet seem so delicate, the heel was high; far too high for the long grass.

"Hello?" C.C. called again and left her bag on the veranda. "They are around here somewhere," she assured Heather. "Hello?"

Buddy was the first to emerge, walking with her head down, along the path that led up from the dock. She looked troubled but forced herself to smile when she saw them. She walked forward and hugged her sister warmly, and then Heather, without thinking.

"Hi, I'm Buddy, C.C.'s big sister. And you must be Mi . . . Heather."

Carol arrived just in time to diffuse the awkwardness. "Hi, I'm Carol, C.C.'s big brother's wife. Can I help you to settle in? Show you to your room, pour you a drink, or get Gloria's pipe?" She meant it kindly but it just seemed to unsettle Heather even more.

"Where are Mother and Gloria?" C.C. asked after hugging Carol.

"Napping. Gloria has a big evening planned. She had Johnnie and Norm set up the projection screen by the boat house, and they're all going to watch old home movies."

"Oh, God. Do we have to?"

"It's just for her, your mom, and the kids. The rest of us are going to the island, and Gloria says we're to stay there until everyone's asleep."

"Any word on when Dad is getting here?" C.C. asked, and for a moment looked so unsure of herself that even Heather noticed.

"Tomorrow," Carol said as offhandedly as she could and took both women by the arms. "C'mon, let's get you two unpacked so you can start having fun because that is what your big brother is insisting on: 'We're all going to have a good time, God damn it.'"

"He's not so bad," she reassured Heather, who was looking more concerned. "Coming?"

Poor Heather looked like she would have preferred to be anywhere else.

"Don't worry. They're not the worst family in the world." Carol reached out her hand. "Come on, you can't stay here all weekend."

≈

"I think Gigi might be dying, but we're not supposed to know," Joey said without looking up.

He was sitting on the dock, whittling a stick with the long, sharp Bowie knife. His mother had been nervous about him carrying it around, but his father was finally okay with it—after he had given Joey the let's-be-careful talk.

He and Susie had finally found some time and space to themselves after spending most of the day with their younger cousins. They didn't mind, but they always had to be careful and not say all that they were really thinking.

"I overheard her on the veranda, talking with Grandma," Joey continued like saying it aloud was helping him make sense of it.

"I dunno," Susie answered as she sat beside him, shoulder-to-shoulder. Even though Joey was older, Susie always acted like she was trying to help him sort out his feelings. "She doesn't seem like she's dying. I think it has to be about something else. I think it might have to do with Granddad."

"Why else do you think he is coming, dummy? I mean, we've never seen him before. It must be because of Gigi." Joey hunched his shoulders the way he did when he didn't know what else to do.

"Yeah, I suppose so," Susie agreed. "It's just so weird. And I also heard Gigi tell Aunt Buddy that it was Grandma's problem to deal with. And she said that the weekend was not going to be about Grandma and all her years of bitching and complaining. But then Mom came along, and I didn't get to hear anymore."

Their mother had noticed her listening and had taken Susie aside. She had told her not to worry—that everybody was just sorting out their feelings the best they could. She had held Susie at arm's length and looked in her eyes to check if she was okay. Susie had smiled back. She wasn't, but she didn't want her mother to be worried about her. Besides, they were going out in the canoes tomorrow; she could wait and talk about it then.

"It's so weird hearing Gigi talk about Grandma like that," Joey continued because he had to talk to someone about it. No one ever really explained all the stuff about their grandparents. Growing up, it was the one thing their father didn't like to talk about. "Stuff happens," he would say and deflect them. Joey had figured that out, but usually went along with it.

"And," he continued, trying to sound like he understood. "Mom says it's good that somebody does it, but it's still weird. I mean, Grandma has hated him all this time, but I guess if Gigi is dying . . . I mean it must be so weird for Dad that his father went off and started another family that he has never even met. Has he said anything to you?"

"Not much, but he did say that we'd all talk about it tomorrow. You know the way he gets. And he said we shouldn't worry about it until then."

"Yeah," but Joey wasn't so sure. Adults were always saying that they'd talk about stuff later, but they never really did. And in the meantime, Joey could see that it was bothering them all. "Dad also said it was just the type of stuff that families have to go through."

"Do you think he and Mom would ever end up like that?"

Joey paused and stared across at the island. Nobody could be really sure. They both had friends whose parents had separated. It was happening all around them.

"I don't think so."

"No. I don't either."

Chapter 4

After the sun had set and the burnished skies had turned from crimson to indigo, the images from summers long passed flickered and danced on the grainy wall of the boat house. Johnnie, Buddy, and little C.C., all as young as Dwayne and Brad and much younger than Joey or Susie, traipsed around like extras in a Charlie Chaplin movie while their own children sat and laughed or rose to mimic their jerky movements. Gloria smiled along with them, but Mary was quiet except for an occasional sniff and twitch and a few muttered comments about how great life had been before "that man" had ruined it on all of them.

Gloria looked over each time she said it, and each time decided to let it pass—for now. There was so much that Mary had to come to terms with, and there was so little time left. Instead, Gloria watched the flickering shadows on her great-grandchildren's faces. She had seen the movies hundreds of times. She knew every frame by heart but still marvelled at the relentless passage of time, measured by the whirring of the reels as each child grew, some into brightness and happiness and some into shadows and doubt. And for the thousandth time, she wished that she could just rewind to the beginning and change so many things.

Back then she had always tried to act with the assured certainty that motherhood demanded, but privately she had always been so full of doubts—so afraid that anything she did would only make things worse. She had often thought that life was so unfair—that it only gave you the wisdom after you had made the mistake. Still, she had gained enough to now know that while she might never be able to correct the past, she could try to lay it to rest so that it wouldn't haunt her family anymore.

By the time the last reel ran out and fluttered until Joey turned the projector off, Dwayne and Brad were tired out and a little cranky. Mary wanted to take them to their beds, but Joey had taken one under each arm and they all waddled off, making a six-legged game of it.

Susie lingered for a while, tidying away the projector, the s'more-stained plates, and the sticky juice cups. Then she checked to see if Gloria needed anything else. She seemed a little disappointed when Gloria said no but smiled like she understood.

"Your grandmother and I are going to sit here for a while and watch the stars," Gloria explained and smiled back. "You go along now with your brother and watch one of your movies. We will call you if we need anything.

"She is such an angel," Gloria added after Susie had stepped away. She knew that Mary didn't think so, but now that they were alone it was time to try to prod her daughter-in-law. She didn't want to be mean about it. She only wanted to try to help her out of the haze of distortions she had hidden in since Jake had left her.

"It is such a pleasure to have family around. Isn't it, Mary? Sometimes we get so caught up in all that is wrong with the world that we forget about what is really important."

"Yes," Mary agreed somewhat distractedly, like she was considering her next move in the never-ending game she and Gloria had been locked in for years. "But I still say that all of this is far too much for you. Think what it would do to the children if they were to wake up and find you dead in the morning. Because that is what you are doing, you know? You are rushing yourself into the grave, and I am the one who is going to have to try to explain it to everyone."

"Mary," Gloria interrupted as politely and as patiently as she could. "I am not the one who is dying."

"Oh?"

"It's Jake."

Mary twitched a few times, but not the way she usually did. This time it was more like she was really trying to keep control of her face. And when she was finally composed enough, she sniffed again. "I see."

Gloria watched and waited. Mary would probably have a lot more to say on the matter. But for now, she just sat in silence except for the occasional twitch. She probably wasn't feeling too much sadness for Jake, and not because she was so hard-hearted. Mary's heart had just grown so full of umbrage and resentment. And she was probably trying to figure out how she should act around the others. She couldn't go on as she had, disparaging their father every opportunity she got. At least for this weekend, she would have to share the mantle of victimhood that she had worn so tightly all these years. A dying Jake's cause would deserve, at least, some sympathy and attention.

"Is it for certain?" Mary finally asked unsurely.

"Yes, I am afraid it is. He has been diagnosed with stage three and has decided to forego the treatment."

"Do you not think that he should have talked with his children before deciding something like that?"

"No, Mary, I don't. And as a matter of fact, I think I agree with him. Even with treatment, his chances would be so slim. What would be gained by putting himself through all of that?"

"He will die," she added after Mary had given her that look—the one she used to say that Gloria could never be impartial where Jake was concerned. "And I think he should be allowed to die with some dignity left intact."

Mary didn't answer but sniffed a few more times, but differently from before, almost like she was trying to hold on to her swirling emotions.

"Do any of the children know?" she finally managed.

"Johnnie does, but Jake asked that he be allowed to tell Buddy and C.C. himself."

"Did he not even stop to consider what this might do to them?"

"Really, Mary? They will have to deal with his death regardless of how they find out."

Gloria sat for a while and nodded in agreement with her own statement, then slowly reached under her chair and pulled out her tin box. She picked out her pipe and filled it with fresh pungent herb. She lit it without looking at Mary and blew a long stream of smoke up towards the night sky where stars were beginning to peep out of the deepening darkness. It was too warm and hazy for them to sparkle like they did on frosty nights, but they were still so comforting and beautiful.

Many nights, as she sat alone with her thoughts, they were the only companions she ever needed. They never remonstrated with her, though she often did with them. Instead, they just shone through the darkness and watched life come and go. She had learned so much from sitting calmly and watching them.

She took another hit and casually offered the pipe to Mary. Then she settled back in her chair and looked out towards the island where the bonfire was blazing, and she could see the others when they passed before the flames.

Mary held the pipe in her hands. "You know I never touch things like this." But she held on to it like she was waiting for Gloria to encourage her.

"Then, perhaps it is the perfect time to start," Gloria answered while still staring at the island. "It does wonders for all manners of aches and pains."

Mary sniffed at the pipe like a cat. "Are you not afraid of getting addicted?"

"Trust me, Mary; you are far more likely to have a problem with all those pills the doctors have been feeding you for years. And, as you have said yourself, they have never done you any good. Try this, and then you can decide."

Mary looked at the pipe again and slowly raised it towards her mouth. "I hope you are not trying to get me high so I will embarrass myself in front of the children."

"Do or don't, Mary. It is entirely up to you, but you might be pleasantly surprised. I know I was."

Mary thought about it some more and finally inhaled a little and began to cough and splutter.

"Try again," Gloria encouraged. "Only, don't draw so much in until you get used to it."

It took Mary a few more tries before she could hold some in. She took a few more puffs, and it seemed to be having an effect. By the time she handed the pipe back, she almost seemed calm for the first time in years.

Still, Gloria could sense what was churning around inside of her daughter-in-law. The news about Jake would have chilled her to the bone—no matter how Mary tried to pretend otherwise. Gloria knew her far too well. And she knew that the warm embrace of all the lies she had been telling herself for years had been wearing thin of late. All the weaves of rationale she had wrapped around her broken heart were becoming withered and frayed. And now, she would have to face Jake's arrival without them. She would be bare and vulnerable, but she had stopped twitching—and her face looked softer than it had done in years.

"Are you going to be okay?" Gloria asked with real compassion.

"Of course I will," Mary answered, trying to sound indignant. "Only, promise me you won't tell the kids about this?" she asked, even as she began to giggle.

"Of course not, my dear. This will be our little secret."

≈

"No," Heather pleaded plaintively, trying to keep her voice to a whisper. C.C. had gotten a little drunk and was becoming far too promiscuous, even with the others sitting just across from them. "Not in front of everybody."

C.C. had been drinking since they got to the island, and while Johnnie and Norm had a few beers, Carol and Buddy abstained. Norm had suggested that they get high too, but since the others had become parents, they didn't do stuff like that anymore.

"They don't mind," C.C. slurred and reached for Heather again. "Why are you being so . . ."

"I'm just not comfortable . . . you know."

"Oh, don't be such a goddamn prude."

C.C. said it far too loudly and tried to pull Heather towards her, but Heather shrugged her off, stood up, and walked to the edge of the firelight where she stood with her arms around her as if she was deciding which way to turn.

"Is everything okay?" Buddy called over from across the fire.

"Everything is just fine, big sis," C.C. laughed, settled back against a tree, and raised her bottle to her lips. "Just like the rest of my wonderful life—all fine and dandy."

Johnnie exchanged glances with Buddy before he rose, almost casually, and walked over. Gently but firmly, he helped C.C. to her feet and directed her away from the fire and down towards the shore. "Let's take a little walk; just you and me."

"Oh no, now my big brother is getting involved. Now I'm really going to get it in the ear."

Johnnie just laughed and tucked her in under his arm, safe and secure, but forced her to walk along with him. "Let's just have a nice little stroll and try to walk off some of the booze."

As they passed, he looked towards Buddy and nodded his head in Heather's direction. She had moved beyond the firelight and could barely be seen amongst the trees. And as they walked away, Johnnie reached for the bottle C.C. was holding, pretended to take a swig, and handed it to Carol.

"But I wasn't finished," C.C. protested, but only half-heartedly as she nestled against her big brother as she had often done before. "Carol's not going to drink it all on me, is she?"

"No," Johnnie laughed. "Carol wouldn't do that to you."

"No," C.C. agreed with sudden solemnity. "You and Carol have always been great. Sometimes, I don't think I could make it without the two of you." She turned to make a face at Buddy, but she didn't notice. She had stepped in front of Norm, who was looking over at Heather as if he wanted to help.

"I got this," Buddy said as she passed. "You just stay with Carol."

≈

Carol smiled sweetly across at Norm, as though every-thing that had just happened had gone un-noticed. She carefully put C.C.'s bottle where it wouldn't get knocked over and smiled. "So, Norm, are you having fun yet?"

"You know me, Carol; my life is just one big barrel of laughs."

"Oh, c'mon. Things cannot be so bad."

Norm smiled wistfully at that. "I don't know, Carol. Some days, it just seems like life is dragging me some-where I don't want to be. Do you and Johnnie ever feel like that?"

Carol wrapped her husband's denim jacket around her shoulders and leaned forward. "Well, I can't speak for him, but I think that when you sit back and take it all in, life is neutral. It's up to us to look at it from whatever side we like."

"Wow, Carol," Norm laughed to dispel the settling mood. "That's deep, but I don't think Gloria would agree—right now."

"I think she would. Gloria doesn't take things so per-sonally anymore. It is one of the things I like most about her. Life comes and shits on her doorstep, and she just gets up and clears it away."

"How do you do it?" Norm asked after he had sat in silence for a while, staring into the fire.

"Do what?"

"How do you always find the positive side?"

"Oh, that. It is just a matter of choice, really."

"So, people who are miserable choose to be?"

"Sometimes . . . I guess so. But then again, I have Johnnie. Who could possibly be unhappy living with such a god?"

She meant it as a joke, but she could see that Norm was taking it far more seriously than she had intended. "Sure," she added. "We go through our fair share of shit like everybody else, but we always find a way of dealing with it. And so far, we haven't had to deal with anything we couldn't manage."

"Is Johnnie going to be okay with Gloria dying?"

"Yes," Carol answered carefully after she had sat in silence for a few moments. She was losing track of who knew what. "You know Johnnie; he will deal with the whole weekend—no matter how it turns out." She looked down towards the shore where her husband had gone. She wasn't so sure, but she wasn't going to let Norm know that. Johnnie probably would be fine after he had dealt with everyone else's reactions. "How is Buddy holding up?"

"I don't know. She doesn't really let me in on how she is dealing with things."

"Have you asked?"

"Not in so many words, but she knows I'm here for her."

"Are you sure?"

Norm took a quick glance towards where Buddy had followed Heather into the woods. "Not really. Things are a bit rough right now. You know . . . between us. Can I ask you something?" He leaned closer so he could speak softly. "Do things ever get . . . you know . . . a bit stale between you and Johnnie?"

"Oh, Norm, I'm not the person you should be talking with about this."

"Should I try C.C. or Mary?"

Carol watched him for a moment. He was being serious, and he was trying to make sense of things. He had always been like Johnnie's little brother, and Buddy . . . Carol knew far more than she would ever let on. "Okay, then. What's on your mind?"

"Oh, I dunno, it's just that . . . lately . . . it just feels like we're going through the motions. Especially . . . you know. I guess I just miss the days when we had more passion, you know?"

"I think what you are missing are the days when you guys were just a couple. Johnnie and I went through that. Believe me, Norm, after a day of feeding, cleaning, and picking up after two kids, the last thing you feel like is getting passionate."

"How did Johnnie deal with it?"

Carol tried not to smile. Norm always needed to know how Johnnie dealt with things. "He always said that he understood, but I guess a part of me worried that he might get fed up with it all. We talked about it and agreed to trust that, in time, things would get back to the way they were."

"And did they?"

"That's none of your business."

"Do you think it will be like that for Buddy and me?"

"Sure," Carol laughed. "One way or the other."

"What's that mean?"

"It means that you will sort it out between you—or with your new partners." She meant it as a joke but he seemed to take it far too seriously. "Oh, Norm, lighten up." She gave him a playful punch on the shoulder. "You and Buddy will be fine."

"How can you be sure?"

"Because I can see how much she still means to you."

"Thanks, Carol; I needed to hear that. I don't suppose there's any chance you could tell Buddy that we were talking."

"Not a chance. There are more than enough family secrets doing the rounds this weekend."

"There are?"

≈

When they got to the shore, Johnnie sat on a large rock and let C.C. sit on his lap. He still let her do things like that, especially when she was upset. Norm used to ask him if it didn't feel a bit weird, but it didn't.

"So, what's got into you tonight?"

"I dunno. Everything. Gloria dying, and dad visiting, and . . ."

"Still not over Michelle?"

"Sure I am. Why wouldn't I be? Michelle was something, all right, but people move on."

"Like dad?"

"As a matter of fact," C.C. straightened up and tried to sound dispassionate as she turned to look her brother in the eyes. "I never really think of him as my dad." For a moment, she wavered and looked like she might cry but instead, she just shrugged. "I guess it was because I was so young when he left."

She nodded along with that as if it had just made sense to her. "Even when we all got together, I never had the feeling that he really wanted to be here and that he was always far more interested in you and Buddy. I guess he was feeling guilty. I was so young when all that shit went down."

Johnnie said nothing but smiled back at her. He knew she always felt warm when he looked at her like that—warm and cared for. Buddy tried to make her feel the same way, but with Buddy, everything was more fussy and maternal. Johnnie just smiled again and listened to her—like the way a father would.

"Still not saying anything?" she asked when her doubts gathered at the edge of their silence.

"What do you want me to say?"

"That I am still great, and that I am still wonderful, and that somewhere out there is the right one for me. You know . . . the usual pep talk. And, if Gloria hasn't sworn you to secrecy, could you tell me what the hell is really going on this weekend?"

"Gloria is just cleaning up some karma, I guess. People start paying attention to shit like that when they get older."

"Maybe I should try that. Lately, I have been up to my ass in nothing but bad shit."

"Like what?"

"Well, my job for one. Even though"—she puffed herself up a bit—"I was sales person of the year—for the third successive year, I might add—I can't help but feel that I have become nothing more than a tit-and-ass wiggler." She paused and seemed to deflate as she huddled closer to him. "Each year, I feel less like the person I used to be and more like a corporate Barbie."

"Congratulations."

"On which part?"

"When you were little, you always wished that you'd grow up to be a Barbie."

"Yeah, I did, didn't I? I guess it is true what they say about wishes." She shook her head like she was laughing, but he could tell that she had tears in the corners of her eyes.

"And after Michelle . . ." She wiped at her eyes and tried to sound brave. "I wished for someone new and fresh. Someone who would look at me and see all the good stuff."

"Give her a chance; she seems like a nice kid."

"Maybe she's too nice."

"C'mon, sis, what's the problem with that?"

"The problem, bro, is that your little sister is still madly in love with the cold, lying bitch that dumped her.

I want to be really here for Heather, but all I can think about is Michelle."

"Ah," Johnnie laughed and squeezed her tightly for a moment. "Do you remember Christie—from my high school?"

"Oh my God, do you still have a crush on her?"

"She's the one who had a crush on me—and still does."

"You're very full of yourself."

"Not really. She called recently for a price on a kitchen remodel. I talked to Carol about it, and we decided to bid way over. Only, that didn't work. She still wanted it. Then I told her that we were swamped and it would be months before I could think of starting, and she said that was no problem. She said she would prefer to wait for proper craftsmanship."

"Oh, God. Couldn't she have come up with something a little less obvious?"

"Carol says that I bring out the honesty in women."

"And what does she think you should do?"

"She said it is up to me."

"And what do you think you should do?"

"I was thinking of sending Norm over, in my tool belt and hard hat—and nothing else."

"Oh, gross. Way too much info. By the way, do you think I should talk with Heather about how I'm feeling?"

"I wouldn't. There's no point in letting her know how crazy and damaged you really are."

"Bastard," she laughed and pinched his stomach. "Only, I'm her first, and I just feel that I should be more into it—for her sake."

"Yeah, you should. But don't worry. You always do the right thing in the end." He rose slowly and helped her to her feet. "We should be getting back to the others."

C.C. nodded but held on to him for a few moments. And as she was about to let go, she raised herself on her toes and kissed his cheek. "Thanks, for this and all the other times."

≈

When they got back, Norm was sitting alone by the fire, now just a pile of glowing embers.

"Where are the others?" C.C. asked as she looked around.

"They took Heather back; she wasn't feeling too good."

"Oh?" C.C. asked nonchalantly, but she wanted him to say more.

"Buddy says she's fine. She said she just needed to get some rest."

"You okay?" Johnnie asked and looked around for things to tidy up, but Carol had collected all of the bottles and cans and placed them in the large cooler—an old green thing that had been a part of almost every summer he could remember.

"Feeling no pain, bro," Norm smiled and held out a can of beer. "Let's have one more for the road."

Johnnie hesitated and checked with C.C. She might want to get back.

"Go for it, and hit me too."

Norm rummaged for more cans as Johnnie stoked the fire and put on a few more small logs, enough to bring the fire back to life for a while. And when it was burning brightly, the three of them sat together, sipping beer and staring into the flames.

"So, C.C., what's new with you?"

"You know me, Norm. Just one damn thing after another."

"Heather seems nice."

Chapter 5

Despite only getting a few hours of sleep, Johnnie had insisted on getting up to drive out to pick up his father. Carol knew better than to try to talk him out of it, so she got the coffee ready and made breakfast for the others. He did stop to kiss her cheek, filled two travel mugs, and was heading for the door when Buddy came down.

"Am I not going with you?"

"C.C.'s already waiting in the car." He said it as casually as he could manage, and held up the two coffees as if they signified something non-negotiable.

"Why is she going?" Buddy asked over her shoulder as she walked behind Carol, but Johnnie had already turned and headed out the door. Carol took a quick glance at the others as Buddy poured her coffee and gathered her composure. She probably would have preferred if Johnnie had told her beforehand and not have her find out in front of everybody.

Not that anybody else seemed to have noticed. Mary and Gloria were sitting at opposite ends of the table, as silent as bookends, each deep within their own thoughts. Jake's arrival was hanging like thunder in the air.

Buddy was never very good in situations like this, and that was why she would have wanted to go with Johnnie. She obviously needed to talk about it with someone, and Norm was no help. He had insisted on coming down before her to see if everyone was okay. Carol had asked if he meant Heather and C.C., or everybody else, but she meant it as a joke. He didn't take it very well, but he was in his hangover trance. He was wearing his old Maple Leafs hockey shirt and sat languidly stirring his coffee and looking like a tired hound that had been out all night.

"You okay?" Carol asked as she fished Buddy's eggs from the pan.

"Me? I'm fine. I just find it a bit odd that C.C. is going. Don't you think?"

"I'm just shocked that she could get up at all." Carol gave her a knowing look and handed her a plate.

Mary looked up at that and might have made a comment, but Gloria caught her eye.

Something had changed between them. Carol had noticed but made no comment as she served them some coffee and toast. She wasn't surprised; Gloria was not the type of person to leave things like this to chance and would have worked on Mary to bring her around. Poor Mary. She was going to need all the help she could get when Jake arrived. But Gloria seemed to have it under control, so Carol decided to leave well enough alone and decided to concentrate her efforts on Buddy.

"Is Heather still here?" Norm asked no one in particular. He and Buddy had hardly even acknowledged each other.

"Down, boy," Carol laughed to defuse things before Buddy could react. Buddy was also a little out of sorts; Carol could always tell. And Buddy had that extra-pained look that she wore when her fuse was burning down.

"She's still sleeping," Carol answered him before turning back to Buddy. "And I think it would be better if you were here when she does come down."

Buddy still looked a little put-out, but Carol knew she was appeased.

"If she does come down," Buddy agreed as she forced herself to smile again.

"Well, then," Carol gave her a quick hug. "We'll need you to talk her down from whatever branch she's crawled out on."

Buddy seemed happy enough with that and took her place at the table between her mother, who glanced at her a little sheepishly, and Gloria, who was quietly watching the two of them.

"And has anyone bothered to look in on the little ones?" Buddy asked, pointedly.

"Yes," Carol answered before Buddy's comment could cause ripples. "Joey and Susan brought over some juice and cereal."

"That's hardly a proper breakfast," Buddy replied and looked at Norm.

"I could take them something?" Mary offered.

"Oh, for God's sake, mother, they're his children too. He can get up and look after them once in a while."

Buddy probably hadn't meant to snap like that, but Carol understood. The whole thing with her father had always been an unresolved mess, and now she was going to have to deal with it in front of them all. However, before Norm or Mary could react, Heather ventured down the stairs. She looked like a kitten, ready to turn and run at the first noise.

"Good morning, my dear," Gloria looked up and smiled. "Come and sit here beside me."

Heather hesitated for a moment, so Gloria patted the seat between her and Buddy. "Come, my dear. Have a cup of coffee and the day will seem so much better. Or perhaps you would prefer tea? You do look like a tea type of person."

Heather agreed to have some tea and sat on the edge of her chair until it was ready, trying to smile and seem as though everything was okay.

Norm drained his cup and rose to get a refill, pulling in his stomach as he went.

Buddy glanced up as he passed and stifled a sniff.

Mary noticed, too, and leaned towards Heather. "I hope you slept well and that you were warm enough."

Even as Carol raised her eyebrow, Mary stopped abruptly as if she was reconsidering what she had just said.

"Yes, thank you." Heather blushed a little and looked back into her tea cup as if she was hoping she could dive in and swim away somewhere.

"I don't want you getting upset over our C.C.," Gloria said gently as she reached over and touched the young woman's arm. "She is not herself right now. She hasn't seen her father in years, so she is a bit discombobulated."

"Yes, we all are," Mary joined in, passing the toast. "And you must try some of this. It is Velvetleaf jam. Gloria made it."

Heather agreed and took one piece of toast and spread a little jam on the corner. She raised it to her mouth and almost seemed to nibble at it. She did, however, smile when she realised that everyone was watching her. "Thank you, you are all so kind."

"We have to be," Buddy laughed ironically. She seemed a little miffed at Gloria and Mary's obvious entente. "We have had to make apologies for C.C. since she was little."

"Now, Rosemary," Gloria chided, but they all could see that she was joking. "Stop picking on your little sister."

"Do you have sisters, or brothers?" Mary carried on serenely.

"No, I was an only child."

"Oh, my poor dear." Gloria touched Heather's arm again. "How terribly lonely you must have been. Still, I'm sure you had the most loving parents, and you never stop being a child to your parents."

"Some more than others," Buddy muttered without looking at anyone in particular.

"Yeah," Norm agreed, but nobody was sure who with. He stood by Buddy's shoulder with the two knots on his pajama chord dangling before him, almost at eye level between Heather and Buddy.

Buddy waved him back and rose and stood in front of him. "I am going to go and finish my coffee by the boat house and enjoy the sun before it gets too hot. Heather, would you like to come along?"

"Sounds like a plan," Norm agreed and stepped forward.

"Sweetie," Buddy stepped between him and Heather again with just the slightest hint of venom in her voice. "Girls only. And besides, after you check on the kids, you should shower and get dressed in case Johnnie needs your help when he gets back."

"Huh?"

"Norm," Carol interjected, as if on cue. "Would you give me a hand with the cooler? It's still outside, and you know Johnnie. If it isn't properly washed and dried, he'll throw one of his hissy fits."

"He was always such a neat and tidy person," Mary offered as innocently as she could manage. Whatever Gloria had managed to do with her was having an impact. "Some wives would appreciate that."

Carol was more than happy to play along—anything to lighten the mood. Taking a deep breath, she turned and looked at her mother-in-law. She spoke patiently, as if she was speaking with a child. "Okay, Mary. I admit it.

I was never good enough for your son, but we're stuck with each other now. Unless you think I should divorce him and take his house and money."

"Don't even joke about it," Mary cautioned and shuddered. "There are plenty of women who would do that without a second thought."

"Yes," Gloria agreed with no one in particular. She probably didn't mean anything by it, but for a moment, Mary seemed to be wondering if it was directed at her and had to be distracted. It never took a lot to set her off—no matter what Gloria may have done to calm her down.

"Norm," Carol called out to him as he sidled towards the door. "The cooler is out back."

"Let him have his coffee in peace." Mary rose quickly like she was happy to have something to do. "I will go and get the cooler." She pulled herself up with a muffled groan and headed for the door.

"Still haven't talked with Buddy?" Carol nodded knowingly at Norm after Mary had left.

"Talked with Buddy about what?" Gloria asked with piqued interest.

"Mary has plans on moving in with Buddy, and this Boy Scout is afraid to say 'boo' about it."

"Oh, Norm," Gloria said quickly before Mary would come back. "You have to speak up. Buddy means well, but I don't think it would be the right thing to do—for anybody."

"So, do I detect a shift in the wind between you and Mary?" Carol laughed and walked over to hug the old woman's frail shoulders.

"I have absolutely no idea what you are talking about."

"Yeah, right. Keep your secrets and mysteries, then. I'm sure we will all find out soon enough."

Gloria laughed, and her eyes sparkled with a little mischief. "You know, you look a lot like Susie right now. Funny, I always assumed she got her good looks from her father."

"Don't worry, young miss," Norm laughed as Carol tried to look crestfallen. "I still think you got it going on."

"Oh, Norm, go and shower. And change out of those pajamas before you make Heather more confused."

"More confused about what?" Mary trudged back in with the cooler and dragged it to the sink. "If you ask me, young people have gotten far too carried away with this whole life choices business."

"Mary," Gloria rose slowly. "Come and walk with me for a while." She took the other woman's arm without further discussion.

"You should go with them," Carol teased Norm after they had left. "And see if Gloria can get your ass out of the fire."

"I can deal with it, you know."

"When? After Mary is dead?"

"Yeah, that's Plan B."

≈

"So," C.C. asked after Johnnie had started the car and she had taken a few careful sips of her coffee. "Why the hell did you have to drag me out of bed at this hour of the morning?" She hadn't really agreed to go with him; it was more like he woke her and directed her to the car. And because she was terribly hungover, she'd just gone along with it all.

"Technically, you weren't in bed."

"Yeah, I figured the couch would be less cold. So, why can't he drive himself?"

"He's flying into Barrie," Johnnie explained as they bumped along the track that led back to the main road.

"What, does he have his own jet?" C.C. asked with her most deliberate indifference. She was a little worse for wear. She wore her dark glasses and had pulled a baseball cap down over her unwashed hair. And she held her coffee cup close to her face as if she was inhaling it.

"I dunno. It's probably his company's."

"Shit! Does he have money?"

"Yeah, I think he's done all right for himself."

"Wow, maybe that's why Gloria wants him here—to cut us all in."

"C.C., there is something you need to know."

"Yeah, like how much is he going to give me?"

Johnnie paused to look at her. She had her tough face on, but he knew she didn't really mean it. "Gloria is not the one who is dying. It's him."

She hesitated for moment before she blustered: "Like I should care."

"That's your decision to make, but that's why he's coming. And that's why Gloria insisted that we all get together."

C.C. sipped her coffee again and turned to look out the window. Johnnie could almost feel what was going on inside of her and knew to let her be. For all of her acting out, she was just angry and confused—he could always tell. She'd always been like that, and there was nothing he could do but let her try to work it out—and to be there when she wanted him to be. But first she would have to get her anger out.

"Oh shit, Johnnie, this is the last thing I needed right now. I'm still all messed up with this whole Michelle thing, and now I got Heather hanging onto me like a virgin at an orgy. Shit, man, when am I ever going to catch a break?"

"Is that where you kids met?"

"Yew, you're beginning to sound like Norm. And that's another thing. Why does he have to get all creepy? Is Buddy not putting out anymore?" Her anger was becoming self-righteous; it was her pattern. "And what's mother's deal? It's like she's sitting on a pickle."

Johnnie waited until the pause was long enough. "Are you nearly done yet, or are you going take a few shots at Carol and me?"

"Screw it all, Johnnie. Can't I blow off a little steam without you acting like my father all the time?"

Johnnie let it go at that, and they drove in silence for a while. He knew his sister, and he knew how to let her come to things on her own. He thought about turning up the music, but he didn't. The mood C.C. was in, she would probably accuse him of trying to shut her out.

He would never do that to her. She was still, and would always be, his little sister, even if she had grown to be a right pain in the butt, sometimes.

"Thanks," she finally decided, having spent enough time inside of herself.

"No sweat."

"I mean for always being like a father to me."

"No sweat on that too."

"For you, maybe, but not for him."

"Yeah, but he's still the only dad I got, even if he was a total screw-up. And now, I just got to be there for him."

"Yeah, like the way he was there for us?"

"It wasn't all his fault."

"Really, Johnnie? Whose fault was it, then? Mine? I was only five years old; what the hell could I have done to him to make him dislike me?"

"He didn't dislike you."

"Really, Johnnie? Don't you even remember what it was like when he came up for the weekends?"

"He and mom had just separated. It must have been so weird for him."

"Except when he was with you—and Buddy. He always had that smile when he talked to you guys, but when he looked at me—it was like he was looking at a stray cat, or something."

"You always were a funny looking kid."

Despite herself, C.C. almost laughed but quickly stifled it and punched his arm as hard as she could, hurting her hand against him.

"And now look at what you made me do, you big jerk."

"Come here," Johnnie reached over and pulled her towards him. "Sure, Dad was very messed up back then, but there's all this stuff you don't know about."

"Like what? That he loved his new kids more than us?"

"Maybe, but the reason he stopped doing summers with us was Mom."

"Yeah, right. Why do you always have to defend him?"

"I'm not. Gloria asked him to stop coming, and Mom started coming instead."

"Why the hell would Gloria do something like that?"

"She was probably just trying to make things right."

"Do you think she was right?"

"Mom and dad were divorced by then. I guess Gloria figured that he was going to move on anyway."

"And nobody bothered to tell me about any of that?"

"It wouldn't have done you any good. You were just a kid. And besides, from the moment you were born, you were destined to become the black sheep. Nothing was ever going to change that."

C.C. had to smile at that and reached up to kiss his stubbled cheek. "I love you—even though you're still a big jerk."

"So, are you going to give your new pixie friend a chance?"

"She does look like a pixie, doesn't she? It's cute."

"I'm no expert in love—or whatever you kids are calling it these days—but I think you have to face it: Michelle is over. Give this kid a chance."

"What do you mean? I could get Michelle back if I wanted to."

"C'mon kiddo, let it go. Besides, you're not the big bad bitch you pretend to be."

"Damn, you weren't supposed to notice that." C.C. sat up and away from him and folded her arms in a huff.

Johnnie drove again in silence as C.C. digested all that he had said. It wouldn't take her long.

"I knew it. Even when I was just a kid. I knew it couldn't have been me. And for years, Buddy was always telling me that I just imagined it all.

"And Mom: she was even worse. When I tried talking to her about it, she just said things like: 'That's the way he looks at me, too, dear. Something has changed that man.' Like that was going to help. Did something change him, or was he always a jerk?"

Johnnie didn't answer, and C.C. waited a while.

"So, you do know."

"No, I don't."

"Then why did you go all silent, like?"

"I'm just thinking about shit. Listen, we're going to be there in a few minutes. Let's get our act together and go meet our dying father like two normal, happy, well-adjusted adults. And later, when we get back, we'll get shitfaced with the others. We're all going to need it tonight."

C.C. nodded as she stared at the windshield. "Yeah, and you're right. She is a little pixie."

≈

When Johnnie went inside to find his father, C.C. hunched lower in her seat. She pulled her cap down so her eyes couldn't be seen. Now that they were there, she wished she was somewhere else, but she couldn't have stayed away. It was the story of her life; especially life with her family.

Sometimes, after she had spent time with them all, and they had gotten under her skin like they always did, she would go home and fret and fume on her own for a few winey hours. Sitting there, in the security of her own spacious and sophisticated apartment, in the enabling embrace of a Sauvignon or a Merlot, remembering and reliving all the terrible moments of her childhood as her confidence melted and trickled away, her mother's voice would start to worm through her head.

That voice was relentless. Everything she had done with her life, everything she had become was little more than a phase—or another attempt to seek attention. That was one of the reasons she drank as much as did, and by the third glass she would get angry and resolve to just cut them out of her life altogether, but that never lasted very long.

While wandering through those sad memories often made her feel so cold and alone, others popped up—memories of sunnier days that could always make her warm and happy and a part of something. Especially when she remembered the things she had done with Johnnie. He was always there, teaching her to swim and all the good stuff that spending time at the cottage was really about.

Buddy, too, and Gloria—they'd had a lot of good times by the lake. And being there with Michelle had made it even more special, showing her the secret little places she had discovered as a teenager who had needed to be alone to try to sort her feelings out. Even showing her where, when Johnnie had helped her build up enough courage, she had jumped from the little rocky cliff into the deep, cold water below.

It had seemed such a height back then, but now it was no more than fifteen to twenty feet. She and Michelle had done it together—one night after everyone else had gone to bed: naked and celebrating all that being young and alive really meant.

Michelle always brought out that side of her—the side that revelled in wild abandonment with no cares about what anybody else might think. With Michelle, C.C. could be like that. But now that Michelle had left her too, it was all becoming so much harder to do.

Still, she felt she had to for Heather's sake. She had to be the one who led them through what Gloria always called "the dance of life." She missed Michelle more than she could ever admit and once again began to contrive ways to call her without seeming so terribly needy.

When Johnnie and her father finally came out, she hardly recognized the old man. She had always remembered him as tall and aloof. Now he was frail and shrivelled, holding on to Johnnie's arm as they slowly approached. When he saw her, he stopped for a moment. He was probably wishing it was Buddy instead.

C.C. thought about getting out and letting him have the front seat, but Johnnie was already leading him to the rear door of the cab. He helped him inside and walked around to put his bag in the back. C.C. knew she should turn around but had to take a peek in the rearview mirror first. He was looking towards her and also seemed unsure what to do next. They might have sat like that forever, but Johnnie got in and started the car.

"Everybody good?" he asked and readjusted the mirror. "You okay, Dad?" he nodded towards his father's reflection. When his father didn't answer, Johnnie turned around to check.

"Yeah, I'm fine," the old man answered and looked away. "I'm just not sure this is such a good idea, now."

"It'll be fine," Johnnie assured him and began to drive slowly and carefully away. "Won't it, C.C.?"

She looked over and nodded but couldn't bring herself to say anything. Too many things were swirling through her. She wanted to turn around and tell her father all the terrible things she had often wanted to say to him, but now—now that he had actually taken form and was no longer a shadow in her mind—she couldn't.

For years, he had been like a ghost that lurked in that void inside of her. The empty space she poured all of her anger and regrets into. That cold place inside of her that should have been warm and happy. But what was the point? He was dying. What was the point of piling even more shit on top of that? Besides, when he was dead, she would have all that new guilt to add to the pile that she could never get rid of.

"Yeah," she finally agreed like she was talking to herself. "It will be just like old times."

Chapter 6

"What is the matter, Susie?" Carol asked after they had paddled around behind the island. She had waited until then because she didn't want her question to carry back across the water.

They had decided not to wait for Johnnie. He had called to say that he would be late, and they both agreed that Carol should take the kids out in the canoe and he would join them when he got back. The afternoon was going to be hot and hazy. It was better to go out before noon.

"Nothing," Susie answered, but she didn't turn around. She trailed her fingers across the calm water, causing ripples. Carol thought about letting it go at that, but something was wrong: Susie hadn't been right all morning.

The waiting was getting to everyone. Johnnie had said they would be late because his father was getting cold feet; Gloria was keeping Mary occupied, but she wasn't at her best either. Buddy was still simmering about Johnnie taking C.C. and while she kept herself busy looking after Heather, Carol knew she wouldn't let it drop so easily. Norm knew too and stayed out of the firing line and entertained their kids. It was all trickling down, and Carol was getting concerned. She didn't want to try to hide her children from it, but she wanted to try to help shape what they made of it all.

She dragged her paddle and steered them towards the island. "It doesn't sound like nothing."

"What does nothing sound like?" Joey asked from the front of the canoe. He had turned around to see what was dragging and looked at his mum like she should have let him know. He was still a little miffed that he hadn't been allowed to take his father's place at the back of the canoe.

"Susie?" Carol tried again.

"It's nothing, Mum. I'm just thinking, that's all."

"You just seemed very preoccupied."

"It's nothing, Mum. I'll be okay. Honest."

"Well . . . if you're sure."

"Tell her," Joey said over his shoulder as he paddled a few more times so they would drift towards the shore. "She's going to find out anyway."

Carol might have reacted to that, but she didn't want to deflect them. Joey wouldn't have said it if something wasn't up.

"It's nothing. I just need some time to think."

"It's not nothing," Joey insisted as he stepped out and waded through the water, hauling the prow up on the shore. "You're upset and Mum might be able to help."

Carol was bursting with pride and concern but kept as still as she could, even when the canoe rocked and nearly pitched her. "What is it, sweetie?"

Susie stepped ashore and walked to the large rock that she had always loved sitting on, but she didn't answer.

"She overheard something Gigi said to Grandma."

"Oh?"

"I wasn't trying to listen," Susie explained, her eyes growing wider as she spoke. "I just heard them."

"I understand. And what was it that you heard?"

"Gigi told Grandma that she had to get honest about why Granddad left."

"Oh!"

"Do you know why he left?"

"Yeah, your father told me when we first got together."

Johnnie had, only not directly. It had come out in dribs and drabs and always with the reminder that it was not to be discussed with the others. Not even with Buddy, who probably knew but seemed to prefer going along with her mother's version.

When she first got involved with his family, Carol had suggested that Johnnie and Buddy should talk more openly about it, but now she knew that would never happen. Their parents were one of the few things that Buddy and Johnnie could never agree on. It always simmered away in the background and when something happened, Buddy would automatically side with her mother, and anything Johnnie did that showed anything less than total support was cause for some kind of recrimination.

Carol had learned to stay out of it. Johnnie was more than capable of looking after himself, and Buddy never really meant anything by it. It was like she felt she could be like that with her brother knowing that none of it got to him. It didn't usually, but this weekend was going to be a test for them all.

Joey walked over and sat beside his sister. Whatever Susie had heard, she would have shared with him and they both looked at Carol as if they expected her to explain. How could she? She was tempted to tell them that it was one of those things that they would understand when they were older, but they wouldn't buy that. Not anymore.

"What exactly did Gigi say?" Carol was curious. Gloria had a habit of saying whatever was on her mind, regardless of who was around. Johnnie always laughed at that. "It is her house," he'd always say. "And she's more used to being on her own."

"She said that Grandma had to get honest about why Granddad left—at least with herself."

"Sounds like something Gigi would say, all right." Carol tried smiling, but they were both looking at her like they expected more. "But you shouldn't worry about it. It's just family stuff. One day you two will have to deal with all the crazy things your father and I get up to." She wanted to make them smile again—or at the very least, chase the worried looks from their faces.

"Why did Granddad leave Grandma?" Joey asked abruptly, almost sounding like his father.

"Who knows for sure?" Carol responded with all the bluster she could muster. It wasn't her secret to tell. She needed Johnnie there now, and she was going to have to stall for time.

≈

Johnnie had walked a few paces away from the car so he could talk more freely. Jake had gotten out too, and was leaning against the front fender. He was in bad shape.

C.C. had stayed in her seat, like she was waiting for a personal invite before she'd join them. He would deal with all of that after he finished talking with Carol. She always made him feel centered again.

"It is far worse than even you could imagine," he said as softly as he could.

"Oh, my poor baby," Carol sympathized, and he knew she was making that shape with her lips.

Sometimes, she did it to make fun of him, but she was always there for him when his family became too much.

She always knew the right thing to say too, and she always seemed to know when to get involved and when to stay out of it. "Take as much time as you need, and the kids and I will go out and float around on the lake 'til you get here. And, looking on the plus side, you're missing all the drama here."

"Is it bad?"

"No, not really. I just said that to try to make you feel better."

"It didn't work."

"Careful, hun, you're beginning to sound like your mother."

"Yeah, and we can't have that."

"Johnnie, even despite your crazy family and the horrible kids you stuck me with, I love you."

"Yeah?"

"Yeah. Even when you get all strong-silent-type on me and repress your feelings. Now pull yourself together and get these people here so the main show can begin."

He smiled as he put his phone back into his belt clip. She did make him feel better. He stepped back to the car and was about to open the door when Jake looked over at him.

"I don't think I can do this, son. Just take me back, and I will fly off and leave everyone in peace. I'm sure that's what everyone would prefer." He nodded towards where C.C. sat as he finished in a tone of total resignation.

"Sorry, Dad, but I am under direct orders from Gloria, and we both know better than to mess with that.

"C.C.?" he called as he opened the door. "Are you waiting on anything in particular?"

"I thought you guys would prefer to be alone." She didn't turn and stared in front of her—with her tough face on.

Jake looked even more guilty, but Johnnie knew how to deal with that. "Git your scrawny little ass out here right now, or I'll put you over my shoulder."

"No, Johnnie, I'm serious."

"So am I."

He folded his arms and waited. Jake was getting even twitchier, but C.C. would break soon. It was just a matter of waiting her out. She was in one of her determined moods and had folded her arms, and when she realized that he was staring at her, stuck out her lower lip. Johnnie shook his head. This might take longer than Jake could stand.

"Right," Johnnie decided and walked around and hauled his sister out and lowered her to the ground. Holding her under his arm, he walked back and took his father by the elbow and steered the three of them into Tim Horton's. After a few crullers and a few doughnuts, washed down by a couple of large double-doubles, all would be right with the world again. At least it would in his world.

It would just take a while. C.C. was going on about wanting a cappuccino, or something, and Jake almost choked on some sugar crumbs and had a coughing fit that nearly rattled the last bit of life from him. Johnnie looked at both of them, but he couldn't think of the right thing to say. He should have brought Carol.

"You may not want to hear it," Jake finally broke the silence. "But I have to say it. I want you to know that I feel really bad about the way things worked out between us all."

Johnnie looked at him as he spoke. His father was unsure of himself, so he smiled to encourage him, but he could see that C.C. was starting to get twitchy.

"I know," Jake continued as though he couldn't be at ease until he said it, "that it's so clichéd to show up like this, but I have to tell you both: You were all worth far more than I ever gave, and I am truly sorry about that."

Johnnie didn't answer. He knew he didn't have to. His father was speaking to C.C., through him.

She didn't answer either and just stared at her cup. Her face was tight, and Johnnie knew she was fighting for control. Hopefully, she'd skip getting angry and just stay sullen for a while. But it wasn't to be. Slowly, she raised her head and looked at her father with withering contempt.

"Really? You think you can just show up now and waltz back in our lives and ease your conscience at everybody else's expense?"

"I was hoping to try to mitigate what was done . . ."

"Mitigate? Like we are some business deal that went bad? You have no right, you know? You can't just drop by and dump your guilt on us."

"C.C., that's not what Dad's trying to do."

"No? All these years he has had no goddamn interest in any of us—and now we get to put up with all this 'I'm dying; have pity on me' shit. This is just too messed up," she added, and Johnnie could see that her anger was going to give way to tears.

"Screw it. I'm outta here." C.C. rose and gathered her things and was about to storm towards the front door.

"The truck is locked."

"Then give me the keys."

"Just sit and wait. We'll be done in a minute."

"Screw that." C.C. turned and marched to the washroom, leaving the two of them staring at the table.

"She'll be alright," Johnnie reassured his father after she had been gone for a while.

"She has every right to be upset."

"Yeah, and she will make the most of it. Just give her time, and she'll cool down enough. Another coffee?"

Jake didn't, but Johnnie had another. Carol always told him he drank too much, but given the circumstances, even she wouldn't object.

He tried to think what she would do if she were here. She knew how to handle C.C. better than any of them. She gave her space for a while and then called her on her shit—but not in a "gotcha" way. It was like the way she was with Joey and Susie. She gave them space—but only so much.

When C.C. finally came out, she looked better. She had washed her face and straightened her hair, and she didn't look so tough.

"All right," she stood over the two of them. "Let's get this freak show back on the road."

"Are we going to be okay?" Jake looked up at her.

"Sure," C.C. shrugged. "Like you even care. You never gave a damn about me before. Why should things change now?"

Jake looked crushed as Johnnie helped him to his feet. "Grab his other arm," he told C.C. as they passed. She might have been reluctant but for his tone. It was his polite but firm way of letting people know when he had enough. Carol always said it was a bit scary.

"It isn't just because I'm dying," Jake announced from the back of the car, after he had regained control of his breathing. They had wheeled out of the car park and slowly accelerated down the road. "I had always planned to say it to you; I just kept putting it off." He almost seemed to choke up for a moment and stared out the window. "And now there is no more time." He didn't turn to look at them, but they could hear the plaintiveness in his voice: a man desperate to be understood.

"I get it," C.C. swung around in her seat so she could face him. "You're dying, and you want to clean up your karma. And I accept that—not happily, but I accept it.

Just don't expect me to get all father-daughter with you. That ain't ever going to happen between us. Go ahead and do whatever you came to do with Johnnie and Buddy and the rest of them. Just leave me out of it. Okay?"

Johnnie watched his father in the mirror. Jake was looking pained but what could Johnnie do? Everybody was going to have to deal with it whichever way they could.

"Okay." Jake finally agreed. "But I will say one last thing—to you in particular, C.C. I wish I could have been a better father to you. It was what you deserved. I didn't mean to be the way I was. I just couldn't handle everything that happened back then. I want you to know how truly sorry I am about all that."

C.C. didn't answer, but Johnnie could tell: his little sister was getting a bit choked up. He reached across with his hand and stroked the back of hers. She looked over and almost smiled but then went back to looking out the window.

≈

"Gloria," Mary struggled for breath and had to sit on a fallen tree trunk. "I know that as far as you were concerned, Jake could never do anything wrong and I could never do anything right."

Gloria smiled and sat beside her. Mary had wanted to stop so many times along the way, but Gloria kept insisting that it wasn't much further. They had climbed the outcrop where the lake narrowed. It was one of the places Gloria often came to find her own peace again, but it had become harder to reach as she aged.

Mary was coming around—slowly and cautiously— but she still needed to be handled with kid gloves. There were so many things they had to talk about before Jake got there, and the outcrop was the one place they could talk without interruption. And if things did not go as Gloria hoped, Mary would still benefit from the walk— or be so tired that she might have less energy for histrionics later on when Jake arrived.

Absentmindedly, Gloria began to clear the area beneath her feet, pushing fallen leaves and other forest droppings away into tidy little piles. It was a habit from her childhood—one that she always did when she was anxious. She never wanted anyone else to notice, especially Mary.

Susie knew, but she could always see right through Gloria. A few times, when she and Gloria had sat on the fallen tree together and Gloria was worried—usually about Mary or the impact she was having on Buddy or C.C.—Susie had made a big show of sweeping the little piles into a bag she had pulled from her pocket. Then she would put the bag back in her pocket and brush her hands clean.

"No, Mary, I do not think that way."

Mary looked less careworn, and even though she would probably never admit it, having a few hits had done her a world of good. She had giggled and laughed as she had not done since . . . Gloria could never remember her laughing like that. Mary had kept trying to insist that the stuff had no effect on her, but even she found that hilarious and began giggling all over again. They both did, and for a little while, they shared a clarity that only a muddled mind can grasp. And for that little while, the world fell away from them, and they were just two women sitting by a lake on a fine evening, surrounded by the sounds of their children, and their children.

Still, Mary would be prone to whining, and having a few puffs of grass wasn't going to change that. She was going to have to find the courage to face her past, and she would have to do it without indulging in all the bad habits she had developed over the years. Gloria understood all of that: it was, she had learned after Harry had died, the sad rite of passage for women who had out-lived their marriages.

"Well, I felt that you used to," Mary said matter-of-factly but with little trace of self-pity.

"Perhaps, but maybe we have all done things we regret." Gloria tried to sound as encouraging as she could, but there was a hint of recrimination. It was unavoidable.

"It was as much his fault as it was mine, you know."

"I really don't think fault matters anymore."

"You say that, but I remember the way you used to look at me."

"And how was that?"

"You always looked at me like I was never good enough for your son."

Gloria paused before she answered. Sometimes truth had to be administered in doses. "Mary, I am sorry if you felt that I was judging you. And yes, I do admit it: I often felt like that. But in my defence, what woman doesn't feel that way about her son?"

Mary hesitated before deciding to be offended and began to sob. Gloria decided to leave her alone for a while. There was nothing else to do. There was no point in saying that it didn't matter now because it did. It had always been the wall between them.

When she realized what an enormous impact it had on Mary and Jake's already strained relationship, she was consumed with guilt. Perhaps that was why she insisted, even when things had fallen apart, that Jake stay and try to make things right again. And even when that was no longer possible, she had him spend a part of every summer with his children. It was foolish of her, and it was selfish.

Only, at the time she had her rationales. She just didn't want Jake to become estranged from them the way he had become estranged from his father. It was well-meant, but it was very stupid of her to try to impose like that.

Jake had tried, but things could not be so easily pushed back together again. When it started to become obvious, Gloria decided that he should stop coming. She made that decision with the certainty that mothers assumed in the lives of their children—an unquestioned infallibility born of the uncontrollable desire to protect and nurture. And when it was proven—not so much wrong as misguided—she had condemned herself for years. But now she saw things differently. Mothers always tried to make the world a kinder, gentler place for children, even if their efforts distorted everything.

"It wasn't all my fault," Mary blurted out when she realized that Gloria was not going to react to her tears.

Gloria nodded but said nothing. She agreed: Jake had been neglecting Mary. He had been so driven by the need to succeed in the world and spent far too much time at the office. Gloria had tried to warn him about that, but even she didn't realize what was really going on. Mary and Jake's business partner had always been close. Too close, as it turned out, and Mary had always been the type of young woman that needed constant re-affirmation.

"You never saw that side of things," Mary added, somewhat hesitantly.

"I saw many things," Gloria answered as impartially as she could manage. "And some of the things I saw were of my own choosing."

"Yes, and you could never see that Jake never really loved me."

Gloria hesitated. Again, Mary was partially right. Very early in their marriage, Jake had grown indifferent to her. Part of it was Mary's doing and part of it was Gloria and Harry's. They had been far too absorbed with each other and the myopic existence they had created for themselves. And in trying to make their situation normal, they had created a world for two. After Jake arrived and began to consume more and more of Gloria's time, Harry grew resentful. He never said anything, but Gloria knew and didn't deal with it properly.

Sending Jake to boarding school was Harry's idea, but Gloria had gone along with it, despite her maternal misgivings.

Not that boarding school was the only issue; it was also Harry's indifference. Gloria didn't fully understand it at the time, but Harry, for all that he was wonderful and generous, had been very damaged too.

It was understandable. He had been through terrible things during the war and had seen so many of his friends die in the most horrific ways. When his plane was hit, two of his crewmates didn't make it. They had literally been torn to bloody pieces by shards of white hot shrapnel. It had been the last thing Harry had seen before his sight was taken, and he insisted that Jake would have to become inured to suffering if he was to be able to find his way through the world. It had been a mistake—one that had cascaded down through the generations that followed.

"He did love you, Mary, only not in the way you needed to be loved."

"And what is that supposed to mean?"

"Mary," Gloria began slowly and deliberately. "It means that, for you, it is not enough to be loved. You must be constantly reassured and, if the truth be told, enabled—especially when you were being dishonest with yourself."

Mary looked like she might start sobbing again, or launch into one of her litanies about all the terrible things the world had done to her, when Gloria took her in her arms.

"Mary, you are loved and you are cared for, even when you make it so damn hard. Perhaps it is time to accept that and let go of the past."

Mary sniffled for a while and then sat back so she could look Gloria in the face. "You have the very rare gift of being able to compliment and insult at the same time."

"Truth is often both."

"And you think I deserve this truth?"

"We are family, Mary, and we have been for a long time. We owe each other some love and honesty every now and then."

"Then you are surely the heart of the family."

"Now, Mary, be kind. I'm just a foolish old woman trying to do the right thing after all these years."

"Very well, then; I will try it your way." Mary sat back and let it all sink in while Gloria waited. She seemed to be thinking of what lay ahead, and her face clouded over. "You know it is going to be very difficult for me—seeing him again?"

"I'm sure that you will manage it."

"And what makes you so sure? We both know how I can get."

"Mary, whatever else about you, you have always been one to put your children first. When Jake gets here, they will need you to show them how to behave." It wasn't entirely true, but it was meant as sugar-coating. Mary, however, must have missed that.

"Do you think I should tell the children how I'm feeling?"

"I am not sure that would be helpful right now."

"But they have such loyalty to me; I wouldn't want that to interfere."

"Mary, they are all going to have to deal with their father the best way they can. Perhaps the best thing you and I can do is to sit back and let it happen."

When the sun reached the middle of the sky and the heat became too much, Mary helped Gloria to her feet, and the two women walked arm-in-arm, back to the others.

Chapter 7

"I just can't help but feel like I am intruding."

Heather sat on the dock with her legs folded beneath her, looking every bit the natural Canadian beauty. Some of the trees behind her were beginning to yellow, like her hair. And here and there some were bursting into red. She sipped some more of her tea. It was her fourth cup, but she seemed to need to hold on to something.

"Not at all," Buddy gushed and smiled her warmest, friendliest smile. She had recovered her composure and was feeling a little guilty for the way she had behaved at breakfast. Perhaps if she were kind to Heather, everything would be balanced again. "We are all very happy you could make it."

"Why?" Heather asked.

Buddy paused to check if she was being snide, but she didn't seem to be. She seemed in earnest, and she seemed genuinely curious.

"Because of C.C.," Buddy decided as she went along, carefully choosing her words to avoid creating new ripples. "As much as we all love to pick on each other, we are still a family and we do love each other. And we look out for each other. This is going to be a very difficult time for C.C. and the fact that she wanted to have you here with her says a lot."

Buddy smiled at that. It was plausible enough, even if she was laying it on a bit thick. She still wasn't totally comfortable with her little sister bringing her girlfriends to the cottage—more for her mother's sake, and her children's—but if that was the way things were going to be, she would make the best of it. And she would put on her bravest and most welcoming face.

"Really?" Heather asked. "But we hardly know each other." She got a little flustered when her own words reached her and added. "Of course we know each other," she laughed nervously and checked Buddy's reaction. "It's just that we haven't had the time yet to form a deep relationship."

"Sometimes," Buddy soothed as her need to comfort and nurture took over, "I think we can put too much emphasis on the idea of relationship and forget about who we really are—don't you think? I know my sister and, even though she is a bit off this weekend, I can see that you already mean so much to her."

Buddy let it go at that and looked around to see if her kids were okay. She wanted to put Heather at ease, not oversell her on C.C.

"You have wonderful children," Heather offered after she had followed Buddy's glance.

"Yes," Buddy agreed, distractedly, "most of the time. But excuse me, I beginning to sound like my . . . are you planning to have children . . . someday?"

Heather blushed a little and forced a smile. "I'm sure I will, but I am only twenty-four."

That was the age Buddy was when she had first wanted to have children, but they had to wait. Norm wasn't ready and—when she was honest with herself—neither was she. They didn't want to have to struggle, and it took a few years for Norm's career to get going. He was still at that college-kid stage, and for a while, Buddy didn't mind. Deep down she'd believed that, given the time and space, he would grow to be the perfect father for her kids.

There were times when it seemed no more than wishful thinking, but she just had to be patient. Marriage was a struggle sometimes, but so far they had managed. "Yes," she agreed as warmly as she could. "I suppose there are so many other things to do before then. Does C.C. ever talk about things like that?"

Buddy wished she could stop herself. She was doing what C.C. often accused her of—'droning on and on about children.' Carol said it was an occupational hazard of being a stay at home mum. She had probably meant it to be supportive, but it always felt like a condemnation—or a comparison. Carol made it all seem so easy, working and being there for her kids. But then, she did work from home. And she did work for her husband.

Buddy and Norm had often talked about him starting his own business—and Buddy would run the administrative side of things, but there was always so many reasons not to. The times weren't right and were probably going to get worse. There was even talk of cutbacks at the office. And the kids were the wrong age for something like that. He had said that he would think about it, but Buddy knew: he wasn't really interested.

"No," Heather responded, carefully. "It hasn't come up yet."

"No, of course it wouldn't." Buddy agreed and then wondered if there had been any hint of judgement in her tone. "You guys have so much living to do before you get to that stage."

Heather lowered her face to her teacup again, but it was empty. Seizing the moment, Buddy rose. "Can I get you some more?"

But even before Heather could answer, Brad and Dwayne converged upon them.

"Mom! He won't let me . . ."

"Will so. He's just stupid."

"Am not. You're just mean . . . and you're stupid."

"Mom! He's calling me stupid."

"Right, you two," Buddy rose and instinctively took the empty cup from Heather's hand. "You are coming back to the house with me, and you are going to stay there until you both learn to behave better."

"Ah, Mom! Do we have to?"

"Yes. This moment."

"But, Mom! He was the one who was being mean to me."

"Well, I don't care. We are going to go and see your father and let him decide what to do with you. I just hope he doesn't get too mad."

"Oh, mom," the boys cried, almost in unison.

"If you like," Heather offered as Buddy seemed to be considering her next move. "I could look after them for a while."

"Really?" Buddy asked without masking her curiosity.

"Yes," Heather smiled back. "You have been so nice to me."

"Okay, boys," Buddy knelt in front of her children, forcing both of them to make eye contact with her. "Auntie Heather will look after you for a little while, as long as you both behave. Promise?"

"We promise."

"Pinky swear?" Buddy held up her finger, and the two boys wrapped their fingers around it, making a game of it.

Buddy was still smiling at that as she headed back to the cottage. She took a quick look back, and the kids were fine. Heather had managed to get them to share the tire swing and was gently pushing them back and forth. They were all laughing, and that, despite everything that hung in the air, almost made Buddy feel happy. But as she climbed the steps, Norm emerged. He had showered and shaved and had no trace of a hangover. He almost looked . . . dapper.

"Right," he laughed. "Husband reporting for duty. What are the orders for the day? Would you like me to take care of the kids for a while?" And even as he spoke, he looked past her towards Heather and the kids.

"Really, Norman, you can be so transparent sometimes."

He gave her that look: the 'I have no idea what the matter is but I will stay in a sunnier mood' look. "I was just trying to be helpful, you know."

"Well, in that case, you could go and check on mother and Gloria. They have been gone all morning."

"Okay, but I'm sure Gloria has everything under control."

"Really? And do you think my mother needs to be kept under control?"

"You know I'm not saying that. It's just . . . well, Gloria and your mother have known each other a long time; I'm sure they know how to sort things out."

"Well," Buddy decided and shifted to her superior tone. "I still think Gloria is being far too hard on her."

"Maybe she is just trying to get Mary to get her act together—at least while Jake is here."

≈

Norm knew he probably should not have brought it up, but the air was getting so heavy—like before thunder— and he had to say something.

"Perhaps," Buddy said like she had stepped back and was trying to consider all sides. "But it's hardly the best way to handle these types of things. She is just going to wind Mother tighter, and then who knows what might happen?"

"I think we all have some idea," Norm muttered and immediately wished he hadn't.

"Really, Norm, do you really think this is the time for mother-in-law jokes?" Buddy looked at him as if she was trying to melt him.

"Shit, Buddy, I'm just trying to lighten the mood a little."

"Yes. That is just what we need right now. My father is coming to say his last goodbye to his dying mother, but you're right. We should all be happy and carefree."

Norm looked over to where the kids were playing with Heather. He had wanted to join them, but he knew what everyone would say. "Shit. I just can't do anything right by you anymore. Can I?"

Buddy folded her arms and put on her injured face. He knew them all by now, and this one always meant trouble. "Have you given any more thought to what we should do about mother?"

Norm could have kicked himself; he'd walked right into that one. "I have."

His voice wavered a little as he tried to scramble back to higher ground. "And I was just wondering if it might not be too much to deal with. We are already stretched just trying to cope with the kids' schedules."

"Then we will just have to rearrange our schedules so we can all be more accommodating."

He knew where this was heading. He was going to have to rearrange his schedule and look after the kids while she took care of her mother. "I don't know," he ventured, unsure where to take it next. She had that look she wore when she was speaking for the family, and he was the one at odds with the flow.

She had started doing it after they had only been together for a few months. One day it was just the two of them facing the prospect of a life together, agreeing on some things and mildly disagreeing on others. Then, without a warning, it became a threesome: him, her, and their relationship. It quietly moved in and became the deciding vote in all their decisions, and only she could speak on its behalf. He had complained flippantly about that, but she always gave him that look—the one women use when they are letting their husbands know that they are being immature.

Then, over time, their relationship sided with her against all the things that had made up his life: football Sundays, beer runs, and watching TV with no pants on. And where they had often enjoyed sex just for the sake of it, their relationship began to demand that there be more romance.

Sometimes, when his frustration began to boil over, she would make it seem like she was secretly on his side and that it was their relationship that was uncompromising. And, as the woman, it was her responsibility to steer them through the maze of it all. He had even talked to Johnnie about it, but he just laughed and said it was the threesome no man wanted.

"You can't expect me to just turn my back on my own mother because it might be inconvenient for us," Buddy demanded with her hands on her hips. And even though her tone sounded like a question, he probably should have just nodded and let it go at that, but he didn't.

"I dunno. I was just talking with Johnnie and Carol and they seem to think . . ."

"Think what, exactly? That we should turn our backs on her?"

"No. They were just saying that it might be better to put her in a home where she could be properly looked after. You know—she does have all those health issues."

"I see," Buddy finally answered in a voice that sounded like it had been dipped in frost. "So, you do not think that I am capable of looking after my own mother. I see. Well, thank you so much for that vote of confidence."

They stood for a while in a frozen silence as around them, the lake sparkled in the swelter, their kids played by the dock, and even Heather seemed relaxed.

"You know I didn't mean it like that."

"Do I, Norm? What else could it mean? You know it's all very well for Johnnie and Carol—he never took mother's side. And Carol—she has no idea what it is like to have a mother that can't take care of herself. But you! I thought you would understand."

"I do," Norm protested softly and felt the ground begin to give away beneath him. "I just think we should talk about it and know exactly what we are getting ourselves into."

"Getting ourselves into? Can you even hear yourself? This is my mother we are talking about. My mother: the woman who devoted her life to her children. And for what? For a son who sides with his absentee father and C.C . . . let's not even go there."

Norm decided to let it go at that. There was no point in talking when she was in this mood. She didn't even believe it herself. It was reflex. "Maybe I should go over and check on the kids?"

"The kids or Heather?"

"Whatever."

"What do you mean whatever?"

He didn't answer and just slowly walked away.

"Norm?" She called after him, and her voice sounded less sure.

She always got like that after she had blustered for a while. Normally, he would go back and reassure her. He would tell her that he understood and that no, it didn't change anything between them, that he still loved her, and he thought she was a good mother and a great wife. But this time, he didn't. And while it felt vindictive, it also felt vindicating.

She raised herself up and called to him again, but he didn't turn back.

≈

Carol sat on the dock as Joey and Susie paddled off together, Joey in the back for power strokes while his sister steered somewhat aimlessly back towards the island. They needed some more time alone to try to sort things out, and Carol needed to let them. She hadn't been totally honest with them, and that bothered her, but until Gloria told everybody else, she couldn't. Instead, she sat in the hot sun and looked around.

Heather had drawn Dwayne and Brad in caricature on the sandy beach with a stick. At first, they seemed unsure of how to react, but they were now helping her draw trees and the cottage in the background. She seemed at ease with the kids, and Carol was glad for that. C.C. shouldn't have taken off and left her, but C.C. probably had enough to deal with.

Family for C.C. was always the backdrop to that part of her life that was more about being dramatic than anything else. As a child, she had learned how to act out to get her way, and as she grew, she had perfected it. When Carol had first started dating Johnnie, she had tried to talk about it, but he just couldn't see it. He was very protective of his little sister, and Carol learned to live with that. Over time, after she had become a part of them all, she dealt with C.C. on her own terms. She responded to each of C.C.'s crises with love and support up to a point. After that, she called bullshit whenever she smelled it.

Family meant something very different to her. She had grown up in a very stable and sometimes staid household. Johnnie's family had been so disrupted, and it took a number of years for Carol to fully understand what that really meant.

Sometimes she wished it was different, but she loved Johnnie and, for his sake, tolerated whatever being a part of his family demanded. But, sometimes, she couldn't help but feel that he was a little too indulgent with them all. Her family were nothing like his. They had no secrets and no shifting alliances. They just got on with life in an open and cooperative way. She was one of the lucky ones.

Norm wasn't. Carol could see him and Buddy near the cottage door. And though she couldn't hear them, she could guess what was happening. Buddy had her motherly pose on, and Norm looked a little hang-dog. Carol couldn't help but feel a little sorry for him. He was, at heart, one of the good guys, but he made it hard to see. It was like he was still clinging to the scraps of his adolescence, and that was one of a great many things that could get under Buddy's skin.

Buddy was a good person too, but she was confused. She knew what was right, but she could never seem to break free of the patterns she had learned from her mother. She had admitted as much many times, only Carol knew never to bring it back up.

Johnnie was very different. He always treated his mother with respect and was kind to her, but there was always a very faint hint of derision when his mother started to act out. Buddy often scolded him for that, but Johnnie would just laugh.

Once, when things got heated, he had told Buddy, in no uncertain terms, that he thought she was enabling her mother. They didn't speak for almost two months until Johnnie gave in and apologised—something he was happy to do for his sister's sake and not because he had a change of heart. He had made his point, and how Buddy handled it was her business. He knew what Buddy was like and left it at that.

Privately, Buddy had later confided in Carol that he was right and that she often felt that she should stand up to her mother more, but when someone else said it . . .

Still, Carol liked Buddy. They were just very different and, in many ways, Buddy was like her younger, more indulgent sister. Finding out that her father was dying was going to let loose so many things that Buddy struggled to keep in closets, but at least they would all be happy to know that it wasn't Gloria.

"There you are, my dear," the old lady called out from behind her, as if the very thought of her had caused her to appear. "Perhaps it is time we got everyone together and told them?"

"Everybody?" Mary asked as she also emerged from the track through the woods. They had been out walking all morning and, Carol assumed from the looks on their faces, hitting Gloria's pipe. Mary was even reluctant to make eye contact.

"I think they should all know," Gloria insisted, softly.

"Even the little ones?" Mary asked as she lowered herself into one of the Muskoka chairs that Harry had carved. They weren't quite perfect: a little askew and were quite mismatched, but that was understandable.

"What do you think, Carol?"

"I think Joey and Susie are old enough, but we should ask Buddy about Dwayne and Brad."

Gloria and Mary seemed to agree on that and sat side by side as Carol gathered the others.

Heather seemed relieved when she was asked to stay with the little ones.

"Mary and I," Gloria began after they had gathered, "have something to say to you all."

≈

As everyone wandered off to absorb the news, each in their own fashion, Gloria sat on the dock. There was thunder on the way. It would freshen things up, but only after a lot of clattering and banging that would echo around the lake for a while. The younger ones might get frightened, and Mary would be skittish, but they would manage. For now, she closed her eyes and let the sun lull her back to other days.

Jake and Harry used to sit on the dock when the thunder came. Harry would sit wrapped in his stoic fatalism, and Jake would do everything he could to imitate his father.

Harry was the poster boy for the "Greatest Generation," those who had gone to war and done what had to be done. Then they returned and stepped back onto Civvy Street without much fuss or drama. They took pride in that. They were made of sterner stuff, and Gloria had once included herself in that. They had all taken the war in their stride and gone on to build a newer, braver world.

But as time passed and the generation they had brought into the world grew up to question everything, it all fell apart. Yes, the greatest generation had come home and buried any emotional scars they had—but they were still there. They didn't have acronyms like PTSD, or anything like that back then. Instead they had silent and suppressed despair.

For a while, they could lose themselves in the spoils of war: the rush to the new suburbs, the constant merry-go-round of the latest model of car, dishwasher, or TV. But not even all of that could silence the whisperings. Nor could the years of psychoanalysis, nor the years of pill-popping that followed, the greatest generation's ultimate achievement was their disaffected children.

Jake had been a part of all of that, dropping out of school to go and find himself in some psychedelic haze in California. Harry had fumed about that. "Is that what we fought the Nazis for?" he would rant as he poured himself another Scotch.

Back then, Gloria always took his side. She regretted that now. Jake had only ever wanted his father's approval.

Harry did approve of him—at the back of it all—but the greatest generation could never bring itself to express sentiments like that. "We don't want the boy growing up soft," Harry would rationalize and Gloria would agree, above the whispers of her mother's heart.

Jake didn't grow up soft. He grew up confused, and when life paid him his share of pain, he grew harder and harder.

"Everything okay, Gigi?"

Gloria opened her eyes and smiled at Susie. "Yes, dear, everything will be fine in the end."

She could see that Susie wasn't convinced, so she patted the dock beside. "But I could use some company, if you are not too busy."

"I can make time," Susie said, playing along. They always behaved so formally when they needed each other the most.

"So," Gloria asked as Susie nestled against her. "How are you handling the news?"

"At first, I was so relieved that you weren't the one who was dying, and then I remembered that he was my father's father—and your son. I guess I'm still relieved, but I am sad for you, and my dad."

≈

As Joey tied up the canoe, Carol sat and watched. She had so few concerns about Joey; he was like his father and later, when Johnnie got back, they would find the time and space to talk it all out.

Carol smiled and waved when he looked over and then turned to watch Susie. She had sat wide-eyed as Gloria explained to them all. Carol could see the conflict that was welling up inside of her—concern and relief— and she knew that Susie would go to Gloria once the others had wandered off.

Buddy was in a huff and would need time to sort it out. Carol couldn't tell if she was miffed about knowing, or not knowing. She had flashed a few glances in Carol's direction as Gloria spoke, and Carol had been careful to keep her face as impassive as possible.

No doubt Buddy would have more to say on the matter when Johnnie got back, but for now, she gathered her children and strolled towards the boat house with Norm following dutifully a few paces behind.

Mary, who had sat stoically staring out across the lake as Gloria spoke, seemed remarkably calm, almost to the point of serenity. And when Gloria had finished, she stepped up to hug the old woman before deciding to return to the cottage where she would rest for a while.

"Excuse me," Heather intruded softly and waited for Carol to turn around. "I hope I'm not being a nuisance, but I need to talk with someone." She seemed more nervous than usual and fidgeted with her hair, pushing it behind her ear, over and over. Her eyes seemed to have gotten bigger, too.

"My poor dear," Carol answered reflexively. "What an awful time you must be having."

"Well," Heather answered hesitantly. "I just can't help but feel that I shouldn't be here right now—with everything that is going on. And I was wondering if I should ask someone to drive me to Gravenhurst, and I could catch a bus from there."

Carol was about to suggest that Norm would probably be delighted to help but thought better of it. She would have to do it. She didn't mind.

"I would be happy to do it, if that is what you really want."

Heather looked conflicted again. "I think it might be best, don't you?"

"You might be right," Carol tried to laugh to change the mood. "This family, eh?"

"That's not what I meant . . ."

"I know, Heather, and I understand how awkward this must be. Let's just go inside and call to see what the bus schedule is. They may not run late on Saturday."

Heather looked alarmed at what that might mean, so Carol linked arms with her. "Don't be concerned. If we have to, we can get you back to the city. Johnnie and I will drive you, once he gets back."

Chapter 8

Johnnie phoned again after he had pulled off the main road. He wanted to let everyone know they were almost there, and he wanted to know how everyone there was doing. Carol assured him they were all doing as well as could be expected and that they were all digesting the news in their own ways.

"How are things with you?" she asked.

"Fine," he answered, knowing that his father and C.C. could probably hear every word that was said. "We just got on the gravel road and should be there in a few minutes."

"Okay, then. I'll let you go, and I'll get the red carpet ready."

"Thanks, Babe."

C.C. raised her eyebrow at that. "You guys are so sweet all the time. You make me wanna barf."

"Well, just roll the window down before you do." Johnnie laughed and checked the rear-view again. The gravel road was bumpy, and with the air growing heavier and heavier, Jake was beginning to look a little worse for wear. "You okay, Dad?"

"I'm doing alright, son, but maybe it's time to think about getting this road paved."

"No point," Johnnie answered the rear-view mirror. "It would just wash away in the spring."

"Even with proper drainage?"

"Too expensive, and it would have to be done every few years."

"Yeah, you're probably right. What about grading it?"

"Do that every spring, but we had a lot of rain this summer—just washes the whole thing off to side again."

He checked the mirror again and looked over at C.C. "You doing okay, Sis?"

"Great! Just loving all this man-talk."

"Sorry," Jake leaned forward from the back seat. "It's just that I don't get to do it often these days. My son—my other son—came out a few years back, and we don't talk the way we once did. We try, but there's all this other stuff between us now."

"Oh," C.C. turned, her voice dripping with sarcasm. "That must be so hard on you." And turning to Johnnie she added: "Stop and let me out before I puke."

"Did I say something wrong?" Jake asked after C.C. had gotten out and slammed the door behind her.

"Don't sweat it for now," Johnnie answered as he slowly drove on and watched C.C. grow smaller in the side-view mirror. And just as he was about to turn into the cottage, she raised her finger in salute—and stuck out her tongue. "The mood she is in today . . . I don't think you could say anything right."

"I guess they're all going to be like that."

"You should be so lucky. C.C. is the most balanced."

Jake looked so concerned that Johnnie had to add: "I was kidding, Dad. Besides, we're in Gloria country now, and she rules with an iron fist."

"Yeah," Jake replied as he caught a first glimpse of what had been his boyhood home, and his voice trailed off for a moment. "Listen, son, there is something I need to ask you."

After his father had finished, Johnnie might have sat longer, but Gloria was waiting for them on the veranda, small and bright against the dark clouds that were gathering on the other side of the lake.

She rose as Johnnie brought the truck to a halt. He had come as close to the steps as he could so his father wouldn't have so far to walk. He climbed out and held the door open, and then waited to let him have some time alone with Gloria. She had come halfway down the steps and stood with her arms open to receive her prodigal son. They didn't speak; they just melted into each other's arms, so Johnnie busied himself with the bags until Gloria spoke to him.

"Johnnie, could you help your father inside? I think he should lie down for a while before he meets the others."

It took a moment for Johnnie to react. He was still thinking about what Jake had asked and was all messed up inside. He couldn't let it show, so he smiled and nodded, even as he saw Mary emerge from the path among the trees. She paused when she got to the clearing and stood waiting. Jake looked up and saw her, and for a moment they stood staring at each other as if nothing else existed.

"Well," Gloria finally broke the silence. "Maybe we should get you inside."

She took Jake by the arm and beckoned to Mary to follow. But Mary didn't, and she turned and walked back towards the lake.

"Is she going to be okay?" Jake asked as his mother and Johnnie ushered him inside.

"She will be fine," Gloria assured him. "After you have had a rest, she can come and you guys can talk, or whatever."

"Will she want to talk with me?" Jake asked Johnnie.

Again, he hesitated for a moment, so Gloria stepped in. "Of course she will. She just needs some time to compose herself, and you need to rest. Everything will be fine after that. You'll see."

"Will it?" Johnnie asked after he and Gloria had settled Jake, left his pills and a glass of water within easy reach, and come back down.

"Of course it will," Gloria almost snapped at him. "And you and I will make sure it is."

"By the way," she asked as she sat by her kitchen table. "Where is C.C.?"

≈

When she finally got back, C.C. stormed into the cottage like a tornado. They could all tell that she was just spoiling for a fight. Gloria intercepted her immediately, taking her to one side and telling her to keep her voice down while her father rested. His room was just down the hall, and Gloria said it in a way that had made it very clear that she didn't have time for any of C.C.'s histrionics.

C.C. wasn't going to be so easily deflected and would have pushed it further, but Johnnie shook his head like he could read her mind. "Go and shower," he had said, calmly and quietly as he put his arm around her shoulder and steered away from the others, "and we'll talk later."

It was probably meant kindly, but it left C.C. feeling that they were all ganging up on her and, with no other option, she glared at him and climbed the stairs to her bedroom. She had wanted to stomp on each one as she climbed, but it would have seemed too petulant. She knew what they were all thinking. That she was acting like a spoiled, little brat. They always thought that.

When she got inside of her room, she leaned back against the door and closed her eyes for a moment. She had to gather herself for what lay in front of her. Heather had packed her things back into her little red case and was sitting on the bed, looking out the window to where the lake was calm and flat but mirroring the growing gloom on the far side.

"You're leaving?" C.C. asked in a loud, exaggerated whisper. It was hot and clammy, and her defiant march back to the cottage had left her dusty and tired. Gloria had made a fresh, cold pitcher of lemonade, but after what Johnnie had said, C.C. couldn't back down and have some. She really needed to shower and change her clothes.

"Yes," Heather responded without turning away from the window. "I thought it might be better if I wasn't here."

"Really?"

"Yes, C.C. I think you need to be able to deal with all that is happening here without me being around." Her voice was controlled—like she was dealing with a child. "I don't mind, and Carol has offered to drive me into town to catch the bus."

"Oh, great, and what time were you planning on sneaking away?"

Heather didn't react to that either, but she did take a moment to compose herself. And when she spoke, her voice was still calm. "There is a bus in two hours. Carol said if we leave in an hour, we will have plenty of time."

"Well, that gives us so much time to say goodbye, then."

C.C. began to take her clothes off and tossed them in the corner. She would have liked to have created more of a scene, but that would have brought some of the others up—more for Jake's sake than hers.

"Were you even going to say goodbye?" She asked as she struggled out of her tight jeans.

"I wasn't sure if you'd want to hear it."

C.C. stood between Heather and the window and put her hands on her hips. She felt a bit like Buddy, but she wanted to regain control of the situation. Everything felt like it was coming apart at the seams, and she needed to hold onto something. "I realize that this may not be the perfect weekend for you, but I think you can understand why."

"I do understand, C.C., and that is why I think I should leave and let you deal with it without having to worry about me."

"And did you even stop to consider what I might want? That I might need you here with me?"

"You don't need me. You have your family. Besides . . ." but Heather paused like she was rethinking what she was about to say.

"Besides what?"

"It's nothing." Heather smiled. "Perhaps you should go and shower, and we will have time to say goodbye before I leave."

"Not until you say whatever it was."

"Well. Okay. I just get the feeling that I am only here so that you have somebody to be with. I have the feeling that it wouldn't matter who it was."

"Oh, is that how you really feel?"

"Well, yes."

"Well, screw me for caring."

C.C. wanted to fly into a rage, but she had to keep it down. Instead, she spoke in a hissing whisper, slowly shaking her head for emphasis. "You are some piece of work. You sit there acting all sweet and pretty, but you really know how to stick the knife in, don't you?" And, as she turned away, C.C. threw her arms in the air. "Can this day possibly get any worse?"

Heather was still sitting on the bed when she came out. While she showered, C.C. had time to reconsider. Heather wasn't going to be like Michelle who always rose to challenge C.C.'s outbursts. Michelle would have followed her into the shower and stayed to have things out properly.

"Feeling better?" Heather asked, politely and impassively. She was still sitting on the edge of the bed like she expected the worst from C.C., but C.C. knew it was time to change tack.

"Yes, thank you. And I'm sorry. I have been acting so selfishly."

Heather didn't answer. She just smiled and went back to looking out the window where the lake had begun to quiver as the rippling winds approached.

"And you are right," C.C. agreed and sat beside her on the bed—close, but not so close. "I shouldn't have asked you to come. It wasn't fair on you, but you are wrong about the other part." She tousled her hair with the towel a few more times and waited for Heather to turn towards her. "I know we have only being together a little while, but you do mean a lot to me, already. I know I have been acting all tough and independent, but you can see through that. Right?"

Heather didn't really respond, but she did look C.C. in the eye. C.C. knew the tide was beginning to turn. "Now, I totally understand if you still want to go, but I would like you to stay."

"Why?"

"Because I am scared and confused, and because having you around lets me believe that when I leave here—and all the stuff that is going down this weekend—my life can still be better."

Heather seemed to be considering it, so C.C. piled on a little more. "I know that I come across all confident and like I got my shit together."

"Please, don't," Heather interrupted, but C.C. was determined and took her hands in hers.

"Please, let me just say this. Then you can go."

Heather nodded, but gently pulled her hands away.

"I haven't been able to say this before because I wanted to seem like I knew what we were doing. I don't. I am the one who is scared and frightened, and you are the one who stays calm and sure of yourself. I need you to be like that with me. I need you to make me feel that I can get through this."

C.C. stopped at that and waited for Heather to react. Finally, she did.

"C.C., I don't think I am the person you need right now. This is all still new to me and . . . well, I'm just not ready for a relationship like this. You are a very complicated person, and you are going through a very difficult time. What could I possibly do, or be, that might be of help?"

C.C. managed a few tears and even as they fell she couldn't be sure if they were real or not. It didn't matter. She had to try everything. If she were to lose Heather as well . . . "You could stay one more night? And it might be safer than trying to make the trek through that." She nodded towards the far side of the lake where the first flashes of lightening were crackling from the sky.

Heather didn't disagree, so C.C. reached out to her as the first of the thunder rolled over them. "Just stay tonight, and if you still feel like leaving, I will drive you back tomorrow."

≈

When the clouds were at their darkest, the rain came spattering across the surface of the lake, hard and insistent. Gloria watched from the window as her family dropped whatever they had been doing and rushed towards the cottage. Except Dwayne, who was being an ass and dawdled along, forcing his little brother to dawdle with him. It was just the type of thing that would have set Buddy off, but Joey resolved the issue before anyone else noticed. He was following along the path and scooped up his cousins as he passed. He had them under the cover of the veranda before they were too wet—and just in time, as a clap of thunder rattled all the doors and windows. They would be cabin-bound for the rest of the afternoon, and that would test them all.

"Dwayne, Brad," Buddy called from inside. "Please don't stay on the veranda."

"Why not?" they answered in innocent unison. "We want to watch the lightening."

"But Mommy would prefer that you came inside and watched from here."

Gloria might have interjected, but Jake emerged slowly from his room down the hall, cautiously stepping into the silence that spread before him. Buddy turned from the veranda and stole a glance at her mother, who noticed and tried to smile back. Susie stepped behind Gloria's chair. Joey stood closer to his mum, and Norm looked at them all like he was trying to figure out where he should go.

No one spoke for a moment, and Gloria had to break the silence. "I guess the thunder woke you?"

"Yes," Jake answered and looked around at them all. "I had forgotten how loud it could be up here."

"When you were a child, you used to hide under your bed."

The younger kids found that funny and looked at the old man with growing interest. For the most part they had no idea what to make of him, but that wasn't the point. Gloria just wanted Jake to have some part in their lives, even if he could only be a vague memory.

"Habit of a lifetime," Buddy muttered under her breath.

Gloria would have let it go for now, but Mary heard and looked disapprovingly over. It was only for a moment before she turned back to her ex-husband and sounded genuinely concerned. "Did you manage to get any rest?"

"Yes, thank you. I am feeling much better now. And," he added looking around at them all, "I was a little anxious to meet you all."

"Better late than never," Buddy muttered again.

"Rosemary," Mary said in her most superior tone. "Would you be kind enough to get your father something cold to drink?"

For a moment, Buddy looked crestfallen and a little betrayed, but Norm stepped in.

"I'm Norm," he extended his hand to Jake. "Can I get you a brewski?"

Jake shook his hand and laughed a little. "Thank you, but I am not sure I would be up for a beer."

"I have made some lemonade," Gloria offered and nodded to Susie to fetch some.

"Thank you," Jake agreed and took a seat in the middle of a family he barely knew. He smiled at each one of them but didn't seem to know what to say next. He took the glass Susie brought and sipped carefully. "Wonderful," he announced, as if they had all been waiting for his verdict. "And you must be young Susie that I have heard so much about. But," he smiled up at her. "No one mentioned what a beautiful young woman you are growing up to be.

"And this big man," he nodded towards Joey, "is the image of his father."

He paused to gauge their reactions while Gloria and Mary nodded encouragingly.

"And who are these two fine fellows," he looked over towards Buddy's children. "They can't be little Dwayne and Brad."

The two boys giggled a little, so Jake went on. "So, are my grandsons going to grow up to be famous hockey players?"

"No," the two boys laughed.

"I play soccer," Dwayne gushed, "and mummy says I am the best on our team."

"And I'm going to be the best too," Brad chimed in. "When I'm bigger."

Everyone laughed at that, some nervously and some automatically, but no one knew what to say next, and the room grew silent again. Outside, the thunder rolled again, and across the lake the sky was tearing itself apart. The rain came in sheets and spattered down all around the cottage in a staccato that accentuated the awkwardness of it all.

"My goodness," Jake ventured when the stillness in the room became oppressive. "I hope we are not going to be trapped here forever." He spoke to the two little ones, who seemed concerned.

"Yes, that would be terrible for you," Buddy muttered again.

"It will not last," Gloria announced as she rose and walked towards the window, passing close to Buddy and pinching her lightly. "It will be done in an hour or so, and we will have a wonderful, fresh evening. The adults: Johnnie and Carol, Buddy and Norm, and C.C. and Heather, can spend another evening on the island while I, Susie, and Joey will keep the little ones entertained. Perhaps," she added in Mary's direction. "You and Jake might like to sit on the veranda for a while."

≈

She had presented it as an edict, and that there was to be no discussion on the matter. Carol caught her drift and piled on. "Great idea. And we have all the fixings for a great big barbeque. I'll just go and start taking things out," she added, looking in Buddy's direction. But Buddy seemed less enthused. "Maybe I should stay—in case mother needs me for anything."

"Not at all," Mary spoke up suddenly like she had briefly wandered somewhere far away. "You young people should be off enjoying yourselves while you have the chance."

"Yeah," Norm foolishly agreed and earned himself a reprimanding glance from his wife.

"I will need your help," Carol tried to intercede after a quick glance from Gloria, but Buddy wasn't ready to give it up. "They," she pointed at Norm and Johnnie, "are supposed to be on barbecue duty."

Norm looked at Johnnie, but he didn't respond. He had been very quiet since he had gotten back and had sat by the kitchen table drinking beer after beer. He'd had four in a very short time, and while Carol had noticed, she had let it pass without comment.

"But we are having chicken," she cajoled as she put her arm around Buddy. "And I, for one, would prefer to avoid salmonella."

"We can cook chicken," Norm said, somewhat indignantly and turned to Johnnie. "Right, bro?" But Johnnie didn't respond to that either. Carol might have reacted for him, but C.C. came down and distracted her. "I can help, and Heather will too."

C.C. seemed so much happier now and, when Heather joined them, was very attentive, even fetching their drinks and trekking down to the cellar for another bag of ice.

"Good, then. It's all settled," Gloria smiled at them all. "Let's have some burnt offerings, and then one more night on Castaway Island."

Carol had to smile at that. It was the name Gloria had agreed on with Johnnie and Buddy when they were younger, but Johnnie didn't even look up at that. He just sat there, sucking on his beer. He seemed tired—or worn out—which wasn't surprising since he had gotten very little sleep since they got there. Maybe, after they had eaten, and spent some time deflecting the others, they could slip away and get to bed early.

Probably not. Buddy was still unenthused and looked accusingly over at her mother. Mary was sitting opposite Jake and was settling in for a while. She smiled over at Gloria, who smiled back. They were like two cats that had come to an understanding.

≈

They had. On the way back from their walk, Gloria had insisted that she wanted them to strive for more honesty and equality between them—that they were two women who had been through all that life could throw at them, and that at the end of the day they were family whether they liked it or not. But there was something else in her tone, something that suggested that Gloria was trying to say so much more than that.

It was typical Gloria: she was probably acknowledging Mary's recent efforts to break her old and destructive patterns. And while Mary was a little miffed at that, she was also a little glad. Gloria had always made it seem like she had accepted her as a daughter, but Mary knew:

Gloria had always been disappointed in her, even before things went wrong with Jake. Now there was a glimmer of something else.

Smoking some pot together had changed things too. When they were high, they had allowed themselves to become silly and unguarded, and with Jake's illness looming over everything, they both needed that. But Mary had a few scores of her own that needed to be settled before she could move on. She began by casually mentioning that she felt that many of Gloria's anti-woman comments were directed at her.

"What comments?" Gloria had asked as if she wasn't really listening.

"All the things you have said about women being mean-spirited and all."

"Oh, that. That is because I am a mother of a man, and I get so tired of women blaming men for every stupid thing they do with their lives."

Mary was tempted to revert to her pattern, but she didn't. They were still a little high, and while it had made her giggly, it also allowed her to see the way she had been. It was so different from how she always thought she was. "And I would be a case in point?"

Gloria stopped and turned to look at her. "Yes, Mary. There have been times when I have sat and listened to you vilify my son to excuse your own failings. I am sorry . . . but that is how I saw it. Only, don't take it so personally, I don't think it is just you. It is the way of things these days. Women have convinced themselves that they are almighty, and when things go wrong it has to be the man's fault.

"And, while I am all in favor of building up women's self-esteem, I am not comfortable with it coming at the expense of men. That would just be another dishonesty, and women have enough of those already.

"And I don't mean just you. All women have such a hard time accepting life and all it does to us. We begin to realize that we are losing our beauty and demand that our husbands lie to us and say that we are not—or that they still find us so attractive.

"We get old and want to know that our men still desire us, even over young, beautiful women. We do not allow them to tell us the truth, and then we say that all men are liars.

"And when I say we, I include myself, too. I could not face the truth when you and Jake were having problems. He was my little boy, and I was determined to make everything better for him, even at your expense. It was very, very wrong of me."

Mary could not speak. A part of her wanted to wallow in old umbrage, and a part of her wanted to soar on long-sought validation.

"All I ended up doing was making things worse," Gloria continued and looked directly into her daughter-in-law's eyes. "You see, I still felt so guilty about what happened when Harry died. He and Jake were not close, and when he was dying, he didn't want Jake there."

She had shivered a little as she spoke. "It wasn't as cold as it sounds. He had always pushed Jake to become the best at everything, and they had many fallings out over that.

"But I guess, in the end, he couldn't bear the thought of Jake seeing him so decrepit and helpless. And even though I disagreed, I also understood and went along with it.

"The oddest part was that I never once stopped to consider how Jake would feel about it.

"You see, life with Harry was like that. I was always so busy compensating for all that he had lost that I too became blind to see what was right in front of me.

"I have so much guilt when it comes to Jake, and I let it influence how I saw you. Perhaps, someday, you can learn to forgive me, but for now, please just try to understand."

Chapter 9

Carol decided it would be better if she took command of the preparations for the barbeque and delegated tasks to them all. The others were still trying to find their places in the swirl of family ties like it was a game of musical chairs. The storm was passing and the sky on the other side of the lake was already brightening, but it was still raining and they would be cabin-bound for at least another hour.

She had managed to coax Johnnie onto the couch on the veranda where he had fallen asleep in minutes. He needed it. He was tired and his patience was wearing thin—Carol knew the signs.

Norm was sent to light the barbeque, and Joey went with him to hold the umbrella—and because Norm looked so lost without Johnnie. Mary and Gloria were entrusted with the salad while C.C. would chop and dice. She, Carol had decided, needed something to do to release her nervous energy.

Heather would have gotten a pass, but she insisted on being involved. Carol was at a loss, but Heather picked up a basting brush and began to coat each piece of chicken with Gloria's homemade hickory sauce. She used the smallest basting brush and stood back to admire each piece before she put them in the steel bowls.

Susie was to carry the bowls out as they were needed, but instead she joined in with Heather, taking the next smallest brush and adorning each piece with her own intricate pattern. Carol could see Susie liked Heather, and Heather needed that right now.

Dwayne and Brad were coaxed into looking after Jake. They were a little dubious at first, but he was slowly winning them over.

And Buddy?

Carol felt it was better to let her hover like a supervisor and even asked for her opinion on every decision that came up. Buddy played along but was mildly critical of almost everything everybody was doing, especially when it came to cooking the chicken. "Norm," she had said when he poked his nose inside. "Please do not undercook them the way you usually do."

Everybody knew to keep their heads down like they hadn't heard, except Carol. She hadn't meant to, but she did raise an eyebrow.

"What?" Buddy challenged her but lowered her eyes and sipped from her glass as Carol's steady gaze got through to her.

Carol's eyes followed the glass when it was lowered and then looked back at her sister-in-law. "You doing okay, Bud?"

"Perfectly fine, thank you; all things considered."

"Maybe," Carol suggested as diplomatically as she could. "You could check and see if it is dry enough to set up the tables. Or I could do it later," she added after Buddy had stared blankly back at her for a few moments.

Carol understood what was going on behind that stare. Buddy was starting to come apart at the seams. She spent so much of life girdled by all of her constraints, and every now and then she just had to burst out of them. Only, she always picked the worst possible time.

Not that there really was a good time, Carol conceded as she sought a diversion. "Buddy, would you make a jug of sangria?"

Sangria was Buddy's one alcoholic indulgence. She would sip from her glass with a faraway look in her eyes. Once, as they shared a few glasses, she had confided in Carol that one day she would go to the Mediterranean. She would sit by the ocean, sipping, while the sun set. Carol could almost see her doing it in the reflection in her eyes, but then they clouded over again.

"No. It's just far too much work to get everything ready. Let's just drink wine instead."

"Ah, Bud," C.C. called from across the table. "Please? I'll even do all the cutting and slicing."

"Oh, yes," Gloria added. "It just wouldn't be the same without Buddy's world-famous sangria—and Heather hasn't had a chance to try it yet."

"Please," Mary chimed in. "You know me. I'm not a drinker, but I would like a glass."

Sensing the shift in family loyalties, Buddy finally conceded.

≈

Afterwards, after everything had been eaten, or wrapped and put away, and Gloria had taken the kids to the boat house to watch videos and the others had paddled over to the island, Jake sat on the swing seat on the veranda. His mother had insisted—and in her most matter-of-fact way.

She was doing what she always did. She was trying to control how they all reacted, skillfully stepping back to give them space when they needed it and knowing when to draw them all back in again. She had been like that when he was a little kid, always encouraging him to do better but never getting impatient with him when he didn't. Not like his father. Harry had no patience and always accused Gloria of mollycoddling him.

It became an issue between his parents until eventually, just as Jake started his teens, his mother began to pull away from him. They stopped having the type of talks they once had. And every time he tried, Gloria patiently explained that it would be better for him to take his problems to his father: he was becoming a man and needed a man's guidance.

It was terrible. Every little thing he was going through could somehow be equated to something his father had gone through during the war—something that could so easily be overcome by sheer perseverance and determination. Things, Harry insisted as he held Jake's gaze, that were now sadly lacking in the world.

Over time, Jake stopped even trying to talk with him—he just couldn't endure the old man's constant criticism. By the time he left home, his father had become nothing more than a bitter voice that had burrowed all the way down inside of him.

He had been angry about that for a few years and lashed out at everything around him. It had cost him. He had dropped out of college, got into some bad habits, and ended up in trouble. When he got out of it and took the time to revaluate it all, he swore that he wouldn't allow the old man to rob him of any more of his life.

Instead, he would prove the old man wrong. He would settle down and become something in the world. Mary had been part of that; she was from a good family who were well-connected. But, when his father died and left so many things unresolved, the old man's bitterness spread to him. That was the most enduring lesson of his father's existence and the very thing that Jake had once promised never to repeat.

That was why he had come, he reminded himself as he settled in and tried to muster his energy. Meeting them all had been so exhausting. As was suppressing the waves of fear and panic that surged up every time he thought about his pending demise. He wanted to be one of those people who could stare death in the face, calmly and serenely. It was, the others in his support group had told him, a moment-by-moment thing.

He had gone to them after the initial shock had numbed a bit—after the outrage, and the pleading, and the despair. They had also told him that going to see his family would be hard—but if it was what he had to do ...

When he had sat among them, he had been able to detach a little and glimpse the great paradox of not taking his own death so personally. He could see how his life—and his death—were not just his to deal with, but now, here with those who would become his "survivors," he felt so much like an outsider who was so terribly alone—and afraid.

He stared over at the island. Gloria was right. Despite everything that had happened, it was still better that he had come and that they all had the chance to go through the end together. It would give them the opportunity to say whatever they had to say to while there was still time. Some of the things might be hurtful and hard to hear, but even that was better than leaving them left unsaid.

He was still staring over at his children when Mary came out and sat beside him. He was surprised, but he didn't have the energy to raise any objection. He was worn out. Only, he didn't want anybody to notice.

"I know you must be tired," Mary softly spoke. "But, if you wouldn't mind, I would like to sit and talk for a little while." She didn't look at him as she spoke, but he knew exactly what she had really wanted to say. They both needed to try to find some closure.

He was a little reticent. He and Mary had never been able to have those types of conversations before, and while it might be different this time, he couldn't be sure. It was hard enough dealing with all the other parts of his life that he had messed up, but Mary—she was always something else.

"Yes, I would like that too," he finally agreed when he couldn't think of anything else to say.

Before, when he had been going over the weekend in his mind, trying to plan how he would talk to them all and trying to anticipate each of his children's reactions, he had glossed over how things might go with Mary, and now he had no idea where to begin.

"Well, I certainly think you were a big hit with your grandchildren," Mary offered after the silence had swirled back between them and grew onerous.

"Thank you. And thank you for allowing me to have this time with them."

He paused, waiting from some sign from Mary that this was the direction she wanted the conversation to go, but she seemed to be struggling inside of herself and didn't answer. Another silence settled between them, broken only by the voices from the island and the muffled sounds of the video off in the boathouse. He hadn't anticipated the silences, either, and how nerve-racking they would be.

Truth be told, he had been so conflicted about coming and probably would have found a way of backing out if Gloria hadn't been so insistent—even playing the soon-to-be grieving mother of her only child. But he was there now . . .

"And I need to thank you for something else," he added when she didn't respond. He was trying to find his way to the point where he could say what it was that he had to say to her. He had often tried to plot it out before, but he had never gotten it quite right. He shivered a little as he braced himself.

Mary misread it and rose to get the blanket she had draped behind them. "You are getting cold. Let me wrap you in this."

Jake let her, but it only made what he wanted to say harder. "Mary," he finally managed after she had wrapped him like a child. "I wanted to tell you that I am truly sorry about the way things went between us."

She never looked at him. Instead, she sat back down and looked at her hands that were resting on her lap. "Now is not the time to talk about things like that. You are not well enough."

She almost made it sound like she still harboured some hope that, somehow, he might find a way of getting better.

"I will never be well enough again, Mary. I am dying, and all I can do now is to try to clear away some of the mess I made along the way."

"But there is no need."

Jake wasn't sure if she really meant it or if she just wanted to deflect all the sad memories those words could evoke. But he had to say it, at least for his own sake. "Well, I am sorry. I am sorry I didn't try harder, with you—and with the kids. You all deserved far more from me."

Mary should have said something about that, but she couldn't. He could tell. Instead, she just sniffled and twitched her head a few times. It made him feel like shit. It made him feel that he had backed up his truck and dumped his garbage all over her life just so he could walk away with a clear conscience.

That certainly was how C.C. would have seen it. She always had that look in her eye—like she could see right through him and the whole charade that was his life.

He had always been uncomfortable around her, and she knew it. She knew it then, and it was obvious that she really knew it now.

Buddy was different; she was torn. She had always wanted things to be happy and normal. She had always wanted her parents to get along, and when it was obvious that they couldn't, she had sided with her mother. Jake didn't blame her for that. He didn't even blame Mary anymore; he just regretted how much damage had been done.

Johnnie was the only one who ever got all of that. Even as a kid he seemed to get it. He never made judgements, but he seemed to be able to see all sides.

"When did it start going wrong for us?" Mary finally asked.

He thought of all the placating things he should say but, after some consideration, dismissed them. If this was the end, then it would be an honest one. "Honestly?"

Mary didn't respond. She just nodded her head, even as she nervously bit her lip.

"I suppose," he decided from all the things he might have said. "Looking back, I just wasn't ready. I thought I was—the way you do when you are young. But I wasn't, and I began to realize that very early on."

"And you didn't feel that you could have talked with me about it?"

He couldn't, and he knew that she knew it—even back then. And every time she had come to him, pleading for more and more reassurances, he had withdrawn further and further into himself until he could never tell her the truth. He wasn't in love with her. That was why he hid himself in his work—and that was why he left her lonely.

"Was any of it worth anything to you?"

He selected his answer carefully. Sometimes, honesty could be the cruelest thing of all. "Of course it was.

Only, I didn't realize that until it was too late. And you must know that it is something I have always regretted. It might not have changed things, but at least things would have been said. I was too scared back then. I was afraid of saying anything to you because it always made you more upset."

He paused to gauge her reaction, but she seemed to be holding up well—or as well as could be expected. "I know now that I should have spoken up, but I kept putting it off, and soon the gap between us had grown so wide I just couldn't see any way of reaching you again."

He stopped to consider what he had to say next. It was hard, but he had to say it: "I began to feel like I was trapped, and I retreated. I know now that I should have stayed and at least tried, for the kids' sake—and for our sakes. But I didn't.

"I ran off and made the same mistake, over and over—with my w . . . other family, with my other children."

"You mustn't try to shoulder all the blame," Mary soothed, even as she sat with tears welling in the corners of her eyes. She was wringing her hands, and he knew she wanted to be held, but he couldn't. He could barely even turn his head when she rose and checked he was still warmly wrapped and excused herself. She said she wanted to check on Gloria, but she would be back to see if he needed anything before he went to bed.

As she walked away he could hear her sobbing so softly. He wanted to go after her and try to offer her some comfort, but he had nothing more to give.

≈

By the time she got to the dock, Mary was crying openly. It didn't matter; everyone else was off doing their own thing, and no one would hear her. She didn't want any-body rushing over to try to placate her. She just needed to be on her own for a while—to try to sort out the jumble of feelings that were churning around inside of her.

She sat on the edge like the children did and trailed her toes across the water, creating ripples that made soft little sounds as they disappeared among the stones along the shore. It had been so easy to go along with Gloria and the whole business of being more honest and open, and she did think that the whole family needed the closure that Jake`s last visited offered, it was just so much harder to actually do.

Before, when her umbrage had billowed up from her broken heart and drowned out everything else, she had just been trying to make them believe that she had been the real victim in it all. But, over the years, as her children grew and began to look at her like she was now the child, she had to concede, privately, that a part of what swirled around inside of her was her own share of guilt.

She had found ways to deflect the blame for all of that on him too. Over time, she had been able to convince herself that her husband had turned against her and his mother had contrived with him along every step of the way. But now that she had sat and looked into the dying face of a man she had twisted and distorted in her mind—a face she hardly recognized anymore—she had to get honest with herself. Seeing his face, shrivelling with fear, and doubt, and regret . . .

It brought everything into clear and simple focus. It was no longer about who was at fault or who was to blame. It was no longer about who did what to whom. It was the end, and that filled her with a very bitter sadness, and regret, and remorse.

Secretly, through the miasma of all those years, she had always hoped that a day would come when he would come back to her. He would beg her to allow him be part of their family again and, for the sake of their children, she would forgive him. But that wasn't what had happened.

He had come back, all right, and he had apologised, but he was the one who got to be gracious about it. He had asked for forgiveness for his part in all that had gone wrong and never once alluded to her transgressions. She had wanted to talk about them—she wanted to hear him say that he forgave her for all of that, but that was never going to happen now. And she knew why: in all the time they had been together, she had never once allowed him to reproach her. When he had tried, she had rushed headlong into a frenzy of self-condemnation, twisting everything he said into sharp barbs that she would flagellate herself with.

That was their greatest and final tragedy, and here at the end of everything they had been, together and apart, they still could not open that door. She had wanted him to throw her transgressions in her face and when she had admitted to them, she wanted him to forgive her. But none of that was going to happen now, and she would never know if it was because he was too ill and lacked the strength, or if he had just given up on her long ago.

She looked up at the sky and let loose the tears that were welling up inside of her again. She let them fall in hopes that they might wash away some of the grit and grime she felt inside—and wash away the foul taste of all the resentments she had gathered for years, collected and stored like harvests while her heart and her soul had become barren, stony wastelands.

She cried for all of that, and for Jake, and for all that they had lost. And she cried for herself; she had suffered enough. For years, she had been haunted by the chorus of voices that echoed inside of her. Voices that reminded her of all that she had been taught to believe was right. Stern, judgemental voices that sounded like her parents, her minister, Gloria . . .

She had hidden herself in self-justification, going deeper and deeper until she had become so lost. She had known it all along, but she couldn't help herself. Her guilt and shame were jagged and poked and prodded her awake, night after night.

She could see that now, and it made her cringe. And she had allowed it to fester and grow until it had contaminated everything she was. She had even allowed it to spill over into the lives of her own children. She had to. If they had ever looked down on her . . .

But now the sad story of Jake and her was coming to an end. Forever. All that was left to her was to rise and see it out with as much dignity and composure as she could muster. She would do this for her children and their children. She just wasn't sure how she could ever manage it alone.

She turned when a match flared from the shadows behind her. Gloria sat under a tree, and even in the flickering light, Mary could see that she had been crying. And there was something else, something Mary had overlooked before. Gloria was showing all the signs of being totally worn-down.

Mary had always said that it would happen. But, before, her motives had been less than pure. Yes, she had always felt a growing concern as Gloria aged, but what was more important was that she be seen as the giving, caring one, especially in the eyes of her children. Now in the harsh light of lucidity she could see: she had only ever wanted redemption from them, too.

Buddy had always given it freely and unquestioningly—automatically and without reflection. Before, Mary had always seen that as loyalty, but now it seemed more like enablement—not that she was blaming Buddy. Mary had relied so heavily on her that Buddy never had the chance to deal with all that happened on her own terms. Instead, she became conditioned to defending her mother.

With C.C., it was more complex: everything was. From the beginning, C.C. always had to act out, and her tantrums filled their lives with one conflict after another.

Johnnie, for all that he made himself out to be kind and caring, had often seemed remote and judgemental of her—at the back of it all. And, she had imagined, always seemed happier siding with outsiders, like Carol and Gloria. He had always acted kind and considerate with her, but Mary had never felt like he was really on her side. It seemed more like he was just fulfilling his duty.

"Want some?" Gloria shuffled forward and held out her pipe.

Mary smiled and shook her head. "Not right now, but thanks."

"Are you going to be okay?" Gloria sat on the deck beside her, letting the soles of her feet touch the water.

"I'm not sure anymore."

"Maybe that's a good thing."

"Why?"

"Because it means that you are questioning the way you used to look at things before."

"And you think I need to do that?"

"I think we all need to do that. Otherwise, we would become prisoners in our little cages of comforting lies." She took another hit and offered the pipe again. "When Harry died, I needed to wrap myself in the comfort of the things I told myself. He had been torn from me, and I was raw. I was alone and afraid and had to pretend that I was in charge."

"For the sake of the family?" Mary asked.

"Yes, and for my own. Then, when I needed to become someone else, I found it very hard to let go. I became the larva that did not want to become a butterfly."

Even though Gloria seemed so in earnest, Mary had to laugh at that. "I would be afraid that I would just become an old moth."

The sound of Mary laughing seemed to draw Gloria out of herself. "So, did you and Jake get to talk?"

"Yes," Mary began cautiously. "And I think we may have finally found some peace."

She said it aloud in the hope it might convince herself. There had been so many things that hadn't been said, but they would have to settle for what they had been able to say. It wasn't perfect; nothing in her life ever was, but if she was to find her way forward, she would have to learn to appreciate what she could.

Still, it would have been nice to hear him say that he understood. And she would have liked if he had found a way to say that he still loved her.

Back when they first started dating, he had explained that expressing his feelings was something he had difficulty with. He said it came from growing up with his father, and Mary could see what he meant. Harry was a hard, pragmatic person who had little time for sentiment.

Jake had promised that he would work on it, but the more he struggled, the more Mary needed. She knew that then, but she had convinced herself that she was only insisting on it for his own good.

It wasn't, and when having to constantly reassure her became too much for him, he retreated into the patterns he had learnt from his father. He started to become cold and impatient. Mary had turned to Gloria, who had told her to give Jake more time and space. She seemed to be giving advice, but there was also a hint of condescension, or rebuke.

"Yet, you don't seem to be very happy with that," Gloria commented like she had heard all that Mary had not said.

"I am, but it is so hard to find anything happy about the end of life."

"True, but it is important not to leave things unsaid."

"But what is the point? He has enough on his shoulders without me burdening him with more."

"What else is there? Say it to me. Say it to somebody, just don't leave it unsaid."

"Oh, Gloria, can we not let it rest for now?"

Gloria puffed on her pipe and blew out a long stream of smoke. "I would be happy to let it rest for now, Mary, if you can promise me one thing."

Mary turned cautiously and finally took they pipe that Gloria had offered again.

"What do you want me to promise?" She took a hit and held it for as long as she could. Her throat was raw, and not just from the smoke. She was choking up again.

"I want you to promise me that when this weekend is finally over, and everyone else has gone, that you will consider staying with me for a little while."

Mary hesitated. She hadn't really given a lot of thought to what would happen after the weekend. Jake would fly away to die, the kids would take their kids back to the city, and Gloria would be left alone to sit by the lake to deal with her loss. "You know that I am always happy to help, but is that really what you want?"

"It is. I will need someone here with me for a while."

"And I was the only one you could think of?" Mary wanted to sound flippant, but she was on the verge of gushing.

"Mary, I cannot think of anyone I would prefer. It will allow us the time to come to terms with what really was, and what might have been," Gloria said in a very matter-of-fact way.

"That sounds very ominous. I am to be the subject matter of these talks?"

"In part, but there is something else I want to discuss with you. I will not live for much longer. And when I die, I intend to leave this place to you. You must be what keeps this family together."

Mary choked back her tears. "I don't know what to say to that, Gloria, except . . . thank you."

"You seem surprised."

"Well, I am. I always felt that you never saw me as part of this family."

"Mary," Gloria took another hit and handed Mary the pipe. "You have always been a pain in the ass, and that alone makes you one of us."

Chapter 10

"Does anybody else think it was a bad idea to put Mary through all this?" Norm asked as he poked the fire. The storm might have passed, but he and Buddy were heading for a showdown—it was inevitable—so he may as well enjoy himself while he could. He had filled the old cooler with beer and dragged it over to Buddy's great disdain. They were sitting on the same side of the fire but with a significant distance between them.

The others were all sitting around, deep into their own thoughts. C.C. sat by Heather's feet and had spent the whole evening fawning, laughing at everything Heather said and never missing a chance to reach out and touch her, a gentle caress of the hand or a soft brush against the arm. That was one of the things Norm really liked about C.C.: when she was in the mood she really knew how to let her partner know how much she was into them.

He had tried talking with her about it once—so he would know how to be better around Buddy. He'd just wanted to talk about emotions and stuff, but at the time, C.C. was all high on wine and Michelle and started acting all flirty with him. She'd always been like that—since she was a teenager. Carol had said that she probably did it just to piss Buddy off, but Norm couldn't help himself and always got sucked in. Especially those times when he and Buddy were going through a rough patch.

He never meant anything by it but this time, before he knew it, they were talking about sex and stuff. Then C.C. pretended to get all pissed and called him a pervert—out loud, too, so everyone else could hear. She came back and apologised to him later and said she was just messing with his head, but Buddy still remembered it differently.

She dragged it for months, too, and Carol and Johnnie had tried to bail him out a few times, but Buddy just gave them that look, the 'You have no idea what that man puts me through' look. Johnnie had told her that she looked like Mary when she did it. That really didn't help Norm that much, so Johnnie laid off about the whole thing—except the occasional shot at him when they were alone.

He put a few more logs on the fire and sat back down. Carol was sitting beside Johnnie, who was broodily nursing his first beer. Despite having a nap and Carol's best efforts to cajole him, Johnnie just seemed to be going deeper and deeper into himself.

Buddy was sitting a few feet away from him, staring into the fire and twitching nervously every time a twig crackled. She was in one of those moods.

Norm wasn't sure what to do. He couldn't just sit there. He knew what they were all going through, especially Johnnie. For all that he tried to keep it together all the time, sometimes he'd break down and tell Norm how much it got to him—usually after they had all been together and his sisters had done something to piss him off. He'd shake his head and say that it was time for them all to take a pill. Their parents had messed up: boo-hoo. There was no point in dragging it out, and everyone should just suck it up and get on with their own lives. Then he'd shake his head again and ask how his sisters had ended up like that. Especially because when they were kids, they had all promised each other they wouldn't. It was all patterns, he'd say and stare at Norm to see if he understood.

Norm got it. Johnnie was never comfortable criticizing his sisters and only ever said enough to blow off a little steam. And Norm got that the girls were just doing what their mother had taught them. Only, none of them ever wanted to hear that.

Especially Buddy. Their life together had been dominated by her mother and all of her moods and illnesses, and Norm could never say the right thing about any of it. Jesus! How the hell were they ever going to manage when Mary came to live with them?

He took another swig of his beer and tried to see the bright side. Maybe he might catch a break. It might be just the thing Buddy needed. Watching her mother, she'd realize and . . .

Nay! There was no point in trying to kid himself. From now on it was going to be him against Buddy, their relationship, and her mother. He may as well just kill himself and get it over with.

Or, at the very least, he should blow off a little steam too. Maybe get a load on and goof it up a bit. Things with Buddy were going to be bad. It was inevitable, but at least he had until they were alone again.

Buddy was always so careful about stuff like that. She had no problem letting the others know how she felt about them, but always in a kind of passive-aggressive way—like she wasn't really serious, or like she was just trying to tell them something for their own good. But when it was just her and Norm, it was different. She'd begin by giving him the look, the 'Do we have to deal with this again?' look. And when she spoke, her voice would go all quiet like she didn't really have the energy to go through all of that again with him. Then she'd make some nasty comment like she was throwing down her gloves.

If he backed down, he'd just get the lecture about how he wasn't trying enough, or how he was taking too much for granted, or how it was time for him to grow and stop acting like a child. But if he turned and faced her, she'd go ballistic, starting with the ever-growing list of all that was wrong with him. Even then, he'd still have time to back down, but he usually didn't. Once they had gotten to that stage, he just couldn't care anymore.

He really should know better by now. It always ended with her marching off to the bedroom, returning briefly to drop a pillow and a blanket on the couch. She'd stare at him one last time and go back, slamming the door behind her. Weeks of silence would follow, and he wouldn't get back in the bedroom until he kissed her ass a couple of dozen times—and in front of the others.

"Still," he answered his own question when no one else did, "It probably would have been just as bad any other way. Mary would have probably worked herself up into a right state wherever she was."

No one reacted to that, either, so Norm finished his beer and reached for the cooler. Buddy noticed that immediately and gave him her 'Another?' look. He didn't care; he was going to get it in the neck, anyway. He may as well enjoy the ride.

"Brewski?" he asked Johnnie, hoping to draw him out—and to draw him over to his side. He was going to need an ally, but Johnnie didn't respond. Carol looked up briefly and forced a quick smile, but her head was somewhere else too.

"You ladies okay?" he asked C.C. and Heather.

Heather just nodded, but C.C. turned and looked at him. "We're fine, Norm. Thanks." And as she turned back, she stole a quick glance at Buddy.

"Yes, you are," Norm muttered just loud enough. "You certainly are."

He didn't look at her directly, but Norm could see that Buddy was coming to the boil. He wanted that. He wanted to force her into it while the others were there. He wanted them to see that she was being a total bitch to him.

He stopped to think about that. It just didn't feel like the way a guy should be thinking about his wife—and the mother of his children.

Only, who could blame him? She was getting worse and worse, and every time he tried to talk with her about it, she'd get all puffed up and defensive and ask if he was saying that she was becoming just like her mother.

She was, but he wasn't going to step into that trap . . . again. He had a few times, after the kids were born, and boy, did he pay for it. They didn't do it for over a year. That was Buddy's response to all his screw-ups. No sex!

Later, when they had kissed and made up, she'd explain that it was about trust and that she couldn't be intimate until she felt she could rely on him again. Never mind that he was out bursting a gut every day to keep it all together—the mortgage, the two cars, and all the other stuff that Buddy felt they deserved for all their hard work.

When he complained to the guys at work about it, they all told him he shouldn't take that crap and that he should just walk out one day. They all assured him that she'd be begging him to come back in a week. They always went for a few beers every Friday evening—a few quick beers because they had all lied to the wives and said they were still at the office.

Norm had talked about it with Johnnie, too, and he had told him that he had to figure it out for himself. He'd said that it wasn't just about a guy and his wife; he'd be leaving his kids too, and that was something he had to think about.

Norm did think about that and figured that, sooner or later, he and Buddy would have to sit down and have it out, once and for all. Only, he had no idea how to approach something like that. He didn't even know what it was he wanted her to really hear.

He didn't really want to break up everything they had. He just wanted things to be okay between them. He wanted her to be more like the way he was with her. When she messed up, she just had to cut him a bit of slack for a few nights. A boy's night out. Watch a couple games on a Sunday, more sex—the usual stuff. And only for a few nights—he knew better than to push it.

Damn it all, he decided and drained most of his beer. He really had to start standing up to her from now on, but not in a hard-assed way. He wanted to start dealing with her the same way Johnnie did. He just quietly stood his ground until she came around. It usually worked, but Buddy had frozen him out a few times too.

The last time it happened, Carol had tried to intervene, but Buddy wouldn't budge until Johnnie broke the ice. That meant so much to Buddy, even though everybody else could see what Johnnie was really doing. C.C. always said that was one of the things she loved most about him—that he never allowed his own feelings to get in the way.

"Johnnie," he called over after he had drained the bottle. "Have another beer, and stop being such a fun-sucker."

"Yeah," C.C. joined in and rose to her feet. "And let's get some sounds going."

Carol agreed and began fiddling with the old transistor that always came out with the cooler. She picked up a station that was playing Zydeco. She jumped up and dragged Johnnie to his feet. He went along with it all, but she had to lead.

C.C. stood over Heather and held out her hand. "May I please have the pleasure of this dance?"

"Certainly." Heather rose and curtseyed. All of C.C.'s attention had gotten to her.

Norm got up a little unsteadily and walked towards Buddy. He sucked his gut in and tried to look like she still meant everything to him. There was no harm in trying—again. "*Mon cheri*, will you dance with me?" He tried to do a French accent but he ended up sounding like the little French skunk in the cartoons—Pepé Le Pew, or something.

"Really, Norm, you look and sound ridiculous."

$$\approx$$

Johnnie clearly wasn't that into dancing and was just going through the motions.

"You okay?" Carol asked and looked up into his face. He looked older and more tired than Carol had ever seen him look before. He didn't answer; he just tried to smile. Carol led him back to the tree stump and sat beside him. "Anything I can do?"

He tried to smile again. She had never seen him this bad before. "Talk to me, Hun." She held his hand and watched as he struggled inside of himself.

"It's nothing. I'm just feeling a little worn out."

"Yeah, Sweetie, but I'm not buying it. Out with it."

"It's nothing. I'm just . . ."

"Out with it, Johnnie. You know you can't bullshit me. What's going on in that man cave of a brain of yours?"

He shrugged like it was nothing, but she knew him better than that. It was probably everything—his father dying, his mother and all of her dramas, his sisters being their usual vain and self-absorbed selves: C.C. staring in yet another tragic love story and Buddy . . . Buddy was getting ready to really erupt, and this time Johnnie was just going to sit back and let it happen.

Carol decided to let it go at that. Johnnie would share his feelings when he was ready. There was no point in trying to force him until then. Instead, she sat back and looked around at the others. For a moment, she thought about trying to deflect some of it, but she shouldn't. The weekend had brought all those years and years of suppressed issues bubbling up to the surface, and they would all have to deal with it whatever way they could. She looked around again.

Buddy had her head down. She had finished her wine and was waiting for Norm to notice. She was giving him an opportunity to mollify her, but Carol could tell he wasn't going to do that this time. He was looking into the fire, sneaking the occasional quick glance at Heather and C.C. dancing like they were really in love. He had a very odd look on his face, but it made sense to Carol. She knew Norm, and he wasn't the creepy guy he could become around C.C. and whoever she showed up with. Norm just wanted to be in love again. It was written all over his face.

"Buddy?" Carol asked as she let go of Johnnie and rose. She stepped around the fire and stood over her sister-in-law. "Can I dance with your husband?"

Buddy hardly reacted, but Norm did. He almost jumped up, after quickly checking his wife's reaction. "Don't mind if I do, young miss."

The station was playing country now, old-timey stuff, and Norm looked so cheesy. He wanted to get closer, but Carol stayed at arm's length. Despite everything, she just wanted to try to keep him from doing whatever it was he was planning. Whatever it was, it wasn't going to end well.

The next song was a line dance and Norm knew all the steps, even insisting that they change partners. Carol should have changed with Heather but thought better of it, and C.C. didn't seem to mind and danced with Norm. Johnnie looked over and shot her another tired smile, but Buddy was making a point of ignoring them all.

"I saw what you did there," C.C. whispered to Carol when they had swung out and were close enough to speak without the others hearing. "Thanks."

If Heather noticed; she didn't let on. Instead, she danced with the same studied precision she showed when basting the chickens. She and C.C. weren't going to last long. Carol smiled at her when they were side by side again. "Having fun yet?"

Heather laughed at that and then seemed to get embarrassed. "It just feels a bit weird . . . with all that is going on."

"Get used to it—if you are going to hang around."

Heather smiled again. "Thanks. That's good to know."

Carol might have asked what she meant by that, but the radio was now playing a slow dance, and C.C. wasn't having any part of it with Norm. "I'm too tired," she gasped like she had been running. "I need to sit down.

"Heather too," she added as she passed and took Heather by the arm.

Norm had been following her and now stood in front of Carol with his arms open.

Ah, shit, she thought for a moment but smiled and stepped forward. She let him put his arms around her, but she did turn to one side as he pulled her closer. He was humming along. He had his eyes closed and while the song played, he looked happy, so Carol decided to let him enjoy it while he could.

≈

From a distance, it all looked so perfect. Norm and Carol slow dancing by the fire while the warm glow spread out to Buddy and Johnnie, sitting like yogis in silent contemplation, and C.C. and Heather cuddling together while above them all, clear white stars poked through the deep, dark night.

"I think," Heather leaned back and looked up at them all. "That I just might have been wrong about you."

"Of course you were," C.C. agreed as she filled their glasses again. "How?"

"How what? How did I come to the realisation, or how was I wrong about you?"

"Yeah." C.C. sat back down and leaned over and kissed Heather's cheek. "And thanks."

"Mind you, it could be just the wine talking, but I think I might just like you a little bit."

"And you just figured that now?"

"Yes. You see, before, I had you on a pedestal."

"And I have fallen off already?"

"Don't tease me. I am trying to tell you how I feel. And, as a matter of fact, I took you down."

"Why?"

"Because it wasn't fair of me to put you up there."

"And don't I get any say in the matter? Maybe I liked being up there."

"C.C., I am trying to be serious."

"So am I."

"C.C. What I am trying to say is that, now that I have gotten to know more about you, and have seen you with your family, I think you are somebody I could fall in love with."

"And what was I before?"

"Well . . . you were all confident, and you seemed so sure of everything. I felt that I could never be the type of person that you would be able to stay with for long— that I would just end up boring you, or something."

"And now that you have seen me at home with my dys-functional, neurotic family, you think I'm the one. What does that say about you?" C.C. was joking and moved a little closer. Heather responded and nestled in under her arm.

"Well, when you put it like that . . . but I was thinking of something a little more romantic."

"You're not going to get all girly on me?"

"C.C. I am just trying to share how I am really feeling. I think I might be falling in love."

Heather was getting a little dewy-eyed.

"You know I am going to remind you of all of this in the morning."

"Do, because I never want to forget. Sitting here with you under the stars, warm, together . . ."

She never finished. Instead, she straightened up and gently took C.C.'s face in her hands. She moved her head closer while staring into C.C.'s eyes. Then she slowly turned her head and kissed her.

≈

"Get a room, you two," Norm laughed, but Buddy didn't. She sniffed loudly and twitched her head a little. Carol could tell what was going to happen next. She could have tried to stop it, too, but what was the point? It was inevitable.

Besides, it was better to get it over and done with. That way they could all kiss and make up in the morning. So, when the song finished, she walked back and cuddled with Johnnie. He was watching his sisters closely but seemed to be of the same mind: it was inevitable.

She sensed the same thing was going through C.C.'s mind, except for one big difference. C.C. wasn't going to sit back and wait for it to happen. She was going to do what she always did. She was going to poke Buddy like a fire. C.C. could be a real bitch sometimes.

When Carol first met her, C.C. was still a teen. Carol knew she was Johnnie's favorite and kept her opinions to herself for as long as she could while C.C. pranced around, creating drama everywhere she went. Back then, Carol used to feel so sorry for Buddy, who spent all of her time trying to placate her sister before their mother got involved.

When that happened, things would become all about Mary and all the terrible things life had done to her. Then C.C. would storm off somewhere and sulk until Johnnie coaxed her back, after Carol had dealt with Buddy and his mum. Norm helped out, too, when he came along.

"Why?" C.C. asked with that cat face she wore when she was about to scatter the pigeons. "Are you uncomfortable with public displays of affection, now?"

"There's a time and place for everything," Buddy answered and faced up to wait for C.C.'s response.

"And this is the perfect time and place—or, it would be if you weren't here to bring us all down."

"Not all of us treat life—and death—as an excuse to party like . . ."

C.C. could have let it go at that, but she didn't. "Like what?"

Buddy was also considering her next move but was being so careful. She usually came out second best in her showdowns with her little sister.

"Say it," C.C. demanded like she was on a schedule.

"Say what?"

"You know—your little party piece."

"What are you talking about?"

"You know. When you get all like Mum and make one of your little comments about my 'lifestyle.'"

That clearly stung, and Buddy chose to get nastier. "I don't know which one of the little voices in your head you have been listening to, but . . ."

"Don't try to pin this on me, Sis. This one has you written all over it. Just ask the others."

C.C. looked around, but everyone kept their heads down. Even Heather, who had been glancing around nervously.

"Shit, you guys," C.C. exclaimed to no one in particular. "How long are you guys going to sit there and let her get away with all this crap?

"You know what? Screw it all." She threw her hand up and turned back and looked Buddy in the eye. "Go ahead and do or say whatever you want. I just couldn't be bothered about what you or anyone thinks anymore."

"Like you ever did."

"And what's that supposed to mean?"

"It means that you never cared for anyone but yourself. Not me, not Mum. Yeah, you try to keep Johnnie on your side, but only because you need him to pick you up every time you find yourself back in the gutter. You never gave a damn about any one of us."

"How the hell can you sit there spouting that sanctimonious shit?"

"Truth hurts, eh, Sis?"

"What do you know about truth? You've been lying to yourself since the day you were born."

"Oh, really? And what have I been lying about?"

"Everything." C.C.'s eyes flashed and pushed Heather's soothing touch away. "Every goddamn thing," she repeated and nodded knowingly at her sister in her most annoying way.

Normally, this is was where Buddy would change her act and get all hurt. Then, after a shower of tears, she'd make out that all she was really trying to do was help her little sister, even if it was all flung back in her face.

It hadn't worked on C.C. in years, so Buddy paused to consider.

And normally, this was when Johnnie would step in and divert C.C., usually taking her for a walk, and by the time they got back, Carol and Norm would have dealt with Buddy. They would have spent the interval agreeing with her and reminding her that C.C. really did love her, and that deep down inside she really appreciated all that Buddy did for her. It was just C.C., they would say. She could never show how she really felt.

Carol looked up at Johnnie's face, but it was hard to read. He was watching his sister the way he watched her romance movies, especially the ones he had seen too often. She could feel his breathing slow down. He even raised his beer and took a long swig. She could hear it gurgle all the way down inside of him. She lowered her head again, in against his ribs, and waited.

"Well," Buddy slowly answered like she was about to call checkmate. "Maybe you're right. Maybe it's time I started to tell you some truths."

"Bring it on, sister. I'll even set the mood for you. I believe that you are a misogynist."

Carol had always thought of Buddy as more of a misandrist, but decided to keep that for when she and Johnnie reran the whole thing later, when they tried to find the best way to put all the pieces back together.

"Me? I don't think so. Clearly, you have some warped and twisted understanding of the word, but do go on and explain to us all how you arrived at that."

"You hate other women."

"That is so rich coming from the ungrateful little bitch that I practically raised. Oh," she decided and continued dramatically, like she was sharing an epiphany. "I get it now. Because I was practically your mother, you think you can take all of your screwed-up issues out on me. Did it ever even occur to you that life was no bowl of cherries for me either? Did you ever stop to think about what I had to go through?"

"Didn't have to. You kept us all very well-informed of each and every one of your crises—real or imagined. We had twenty-four hour news before CNN was even invented. Between you and Mum, you guys were like listening to the Financial News on a Black Monday."

"Well," Buddy inhaled sharply the way she had often seen her mother do. "Here's another news flash for you. Some of us are here to say goodbye to our dying father. Or hadn't you noticed?"

The mention of her father made C.C. stop in her tracks, so Buddy pushed her advantage. "Of course you didn't. This was just another chance to bring one of your ... friends up here so you could act like Woodstock, or something."

"Don't give me all that grieving crap—especially for some asshole you barely knew."

"At least he was my father."

"And what exactly is that supposed to mean?"

"You claim to be such a smart ass, you figure it out."

Chapter 11

When the morning came, it was bright but a bit brittle. The summer was waning. The sun rose a little later each morning, and it was taking a little longer to warm the world that waited. The storm had cleared out the last of the summer haze, and all around the cottage, life was bustling to get ready for the coming of winter. Birds gathered and flew in circles, waiting for instinct to decide when they should fly south, while on the ground all kinds of creatures foraged between the trunks of the trees where leaves had already begun to gather, some yellow and some red, and some turning brown.

Despite all that had happened the previous evening, Gloria took a few moments to stop and admire it all. It was so reassuring to think that life would go on, even surviving winter after winter.

It had always been Harry's favorite time of the year too. He would get up just as the sky was brightening and the early birds began to sing. He would make his own way down to the dock, feeling for all that was familiar with his hands and feet. He'd get there just as the sun was rising and grope around for his chair. When he found it, he'd face it towards the dawn and then settle in to listen as the world around him woke. He would turn his head to every sound, but not the way a seeing person would.

Sometimes, when Jake was still a child, Harry would let him sit with him, but that never lasted long. Harry would quickly tire of his son's fidgeting, and before long, Jake would come back with tears in the corners of his eyes. Gloria had thought it better to pretend not to notice them and just let him go inside without commenting.

She remembered all of that so clearly now—and all the other times she should have tried to make things different. She hadn't, and now the consequences had rippled down through all their lives. It was her sad legacy, and she had been foolish to think that one last weekend was going to change any of that. Reconciliation, it seemed, was just far too much to hope for at this stage. They would have closure, but it wasn't going to be the type she had wanted for herself and for all of them. In fact, in the clear light of day, it now just seemed to be nothing more than an old woman's foolishness.

Part of the way she was feeling, she admitted as she forced down the rising wave of self-pity, was that she was just too tired to be more positive; she had hardly slept. She had woken when they had gotten back from the island: Johnnie and Carol, C.C. and Heather, all in one canoe.

She knew instinctively that something had gone wrong, and Carol's face confirmed it. Gloria stifled her own reactions and automatically put the kettle on as Carol and Heather ushered the sobbing C.C. off to bed. Johnnie stayed in the kitchen and seemed almost sheepish. "How bad is it?" she had asked him after they had stood in silence for a few moments. She had respected his need to sit out for a while, but she needed him to get back in the game. Together, they would have to try to put all the pieces back together—whatever had happened.

Johnnie had just shrugged. "The shit has really hit the fan."

He didn't seem to want to say much more than that, so Gloria waited until Carol returned, but just as she had begun to explain, Buddy and Norm had come back. An awkward silence followed until Buddy had excused herself and went upstairs. Norm might have lingered, but Carol had nodded at him until he followed.

"How did Buddy even know about this? Did you know?" Gloria asked when they were gone.

Johnnie had just shrugged again, so Carol had answered. "I think Buddy might have just thrown it out there. It was just the wrong time to say something like that."

"And what do you think we should do?" Gloria had asked after she had heard the whole story.

Johnnie had just looked at his hands. Carol had waited and watched the two of them, but they were at a loss. "Maybe," she had suggested as she rose and took Johnnie by the hand. "We should all get some sleep and try to sort it out in the morning."

Gloria might have asked them to sit a bit longer, but Carol was right: they all needed to sleep on it. She tidied up and followed them upstairs, but as she lay back in her bed, she began to despair. The ghosts of the past were prowling, and there was absolutely nothing she could do about it now. She had done her best. She had tried to anticipate everyone's reactions and the best way to try to deal with them all, but there were just too many unpredictables.

How was Mary going to deal with it? She had just begun to break free of all her old habits and now this was probably going to send her all the way back.

How was C.C. going to deal with it?

How was Buddy going to be able to face them all again?

There was little point in trying to get any sleep, so she had sat by her bedroom window. She had looked up at the stars that were fading in the predawn skies. She had looked down on the still, dark lake, unruffled for a while yet. And while it was all so familiar, it had brought her little comfort.

She might have allowed herself to cry, but she couldn't. She needed to stay strong—at least until the weekend was over. Then, when the winter returned, she would have all the long months of peace and solitude to put herself back together. And it would give the others the time they needed to sort out their own reactions. Perhaps by Thanksgiving . . . or Christmas . . .

So, she sat by her window and waited as the house finally grew quiet. Earlier, she had heard Johnnie and Carol as they exchanged a few hushed whispers, but they soon fell silent. She had heard Buddy whispering plaintively but Norm never answered. She had heard Heather and C.C. too. C.C. had cried and cried while Heather tried to console her. In time, they too had fallen silent, but soon after, she heard someone sneak down the stairs.

She had been about to get up and follow when she heard C.C. speak to someone. She couldn't make out what she'd said, but another whisper answered. It sounded so old and croaked. She was concerned, but knew she had to give them time together—no matter what.

She had waited until she heard C.C. climb back up the stairs and settle back in her room. She waited a few more minutes, then went down and busied herself in her kitchen. Jake was sitting on the veranda. He was wrapped in a blanket, so things with C.C. couldn't have gone too badly.

Gloria waited until the coffee was ready before she ventured out. "It is a beautiful morning."

Jake turned slowly and smiled. His face looked so ashy, and that tore at her heart, but she had to be brave and put on her cheery face. "It is," he answered like he was trying to decide on something else.

"Your father used to love mornings like this."

"Yes, I remember." Jake answered with some enthusiasm, but his voice sounded so cold and impersonal.

"Do you still hate him?"

"No," Jake answered slowly and almost solemnly. "I did, once. In fact, I wasted far too much of my life hating him."

"But not anymore?"

"No, not since . . ."

"Well, that is something. And it must have been nice to see the kids again—and you had fun with your grandkids."

"Yes, and thank you for that."

"For what?"

"For making it all possible."

"We're still family."

"For better or worse?"

"Yes, indeed. Did I hear you talking to C.C. earlier?"

"Yes."

"And what did you guys talk about?"

≈

He hadn't been able to sleep and was wandering towards the kitchen when they had met in the almost-darkness. He could see that she had been crying—and she seemed startled to see him. She had said that she had only come down for a drink. He had laughed nervously and said he was doing the same. She was nervous, too, and went into the kitchen to pour them both some lemonade.

When she came back and handed it to him, they politely agreed to sit together on the veranda, and they sat in silence for a while. Then, slowly and hesitantly, she began to tell him what had happened, and he sat in a total, stunned silence. He had dreaded the day she would find out, and now that it had happened, he had no idea what to say to her.

"So?" she finally asked. "Is it true?"

He couldn't bring himself to answer as she sat staring at him. He couldn't even look her in the eye.

"It's okay," she finally decided. "In a weird way, it kind of makes everything clearer—like the answer to a question I had never gotten around to asking."

"Did you ever suspect?" he finally asked.

"Yes and no. When we were little, the others would tease me about it. They said I had to have been adopted—or something.

"I didn't believe them—of course—and I don't think they believed it, either. But it was always something that . . . sometimes seemed so obvious."

He didn't know what to say, but he didn't have to. She was talking to herself more than him. She said that it was okay, that in a strange way it all made sense now. She might have been trying to convince herself, but she kept looking at him.

"You know," she said to him after she seemed to have let her own words sink in. "In a way, it makes me happy."

"Really? How?"

"Well, you and I never got on, right? It makes perfect sense now. I used to think it was me. It wasn't. It was just more of life's shit. And don't worry; I am more than used to it. In fact"—she forced herself to laugh—"it has made me what I am today."

"And what is that?"

"Tough enough to get through anything life throws at me."

As she spoke, she looked like she did when she was young—when she stuck out her jaw to seem defiant. That used to bother him before, like it was all directed at him. But it didn't feel like that anymore. Instead, she just seemed like she was letting it all out. "I am so sorry," he said when she finally felt silent.

"For what?"

"You deserved better from me. Even though . . ."

"Even though I wasn't yours?"

"That shouldn't have mattered. You were just a kid, and I should have seen what a great kid you were."

She softened a bit at that and reached out and took his hand. "Thanks."

"Can I tell you something?" he asked and waited until she looked directly into his eyes and nodded. "It wasn't that I didn't like you . . . it's just that I was so afraid of you."

"Really? What the hell was there to be afraid of? I was just a little kid."

"Yeah, but you always looked at me like you knew. I guess it was just my guilt."

"What did you have to feel guilty about?"

"Because I was a big part of the problem—not that I'm saying you were a problem. I just felt that . . . well, I should have been a much better father to you."

"Thanks."

"I am sorry for all of that, and I am sorry that this is how you found out, you know?"

"It doesn't really matter now." She answered and kept looking at him in a soft, curious way. It had made him wish that everything could have been different.

"Will you be okay?"

"Yeah . . . I think what got me most upset was that Buddy got to get one over on me." She stuck her chin out again, and he wanted to reach out and take her in his arms. "And she had this really weird look on her face."

"You know . . ." he said as his voice trembled. But he couldn't say it. He had the chance, but he let all his other stuff get in the way.

≈

"So, what did you guys talk about?" Gloria asked again.

"Everything."

"Did she tell you what happened?"

"She did."

"And is she going to be okay?"

"Yes, I think she'll be fine. It's Buddy I would worry about. What on earth made her do it?"

≈

"What on earth made you do it?" Mary asked as she handed her daughter a coffee.

Buddy had crept down while Jake and Gloria were sitting outside. She had ghosted through the kitchen and hadn't even turned the lights on. She had walked right past Mary and had headed out the back door. Mary poured coffee into two travel mugs and slowly followed. Buddy was going to the dock, and they would have time to talk before the others disturbed them. The kids had been up late watching movies and would probably sleep until noon.

"I don't know." Buddy sobbed a little and raised her coffee to her lowered face. "I didn't really mean it. We were just going at each other and it came out. And even as I said it, I suddenly realized . . . I think we all did. Oh, mother, I am so sorry."

"There is nothing for you to apologize for," Mary assured her as she tried to find herself in all that was swirling around her. Her big secret had always been there at the vague edge of everything they were together, and anytime anyone came close to it, she had distracted them with a fit of histrionics. It was how she dealt with it within herself—blaming Jake, blaming Gloria, blaming everyone but herself. She shivered a little as she thought about the way she had been—and what she would now have to face. Her first instinct was to feel sorry for herself and to try to deflect her guilt and shame, but she had to move past all of that. She had to for her children's sake. "And how did C.C. take it?"

"How do you think? She just stood there in shock—it was just like I stabbed her in the heart."

Mary could almost feel her own heart being pierced but forced herself past that. "I'm sure it wasn't as bad as all that."

"No, mother. It was worse."

"Well," Mary answered after they had sat in silence for a while. "I am sure the others are looking after her."

Buddy looked up in surprise, like she had been expecting a totally different reaction. Mary knew which one, and smiled and stroked her daughter's hair. "Don't worry about me. I'm fine, and right now I just want to be here for you."

Buddy blinked like she wasn't sure how to react, but then her face clouded again. "Mother, you shouldn't be worried about me—or any of us. We are old enough to look after ourselves. Besides, you have more than enough to deal with, already, and I don't want you to get upset."

"I am not going to let this upset me. In fact, I have made a pact with Gloria to try and never let anything upset me again—at least, not the way it used to." She said it to lighten the mood, but it seemed to have the opposite effect on her daughter. At the mention of Gloria's name, Buddy's eyes narrowed a little.

"Maybe what we all need is to spend the afternoons getting stoned with Gloria. It seemed to have worked wonders for you."

"Oh, dear, don't be unkind—even if I deserve it. This is not about smoking a little pot."

"Really, mother? Since you got here, you've done nothing but get high and tag along with Gloria."

Buddy was jealous. Before, Mary had always looked to her to take her side against the others. From now on, things would have to be different. In changing herself, Mary would also have to change her relationship with her daughter—and Johnnie and C.C. too.

"Rosebud, this whole weekend has forced me to look at my life very differently. Sure, smoking a little pot helped, but so many other things have happened, and I have been forced to realize that I have to come to terms with all that I have been avoiding. It scares me, Rosebud, and it seems impossible, but even in just realizing it, it feels like so much of the burden I have carried has begun to break off and float away."

"That's what drugs do, Mother, but it is all just an illusion."

"Perhaps, but it is still better than the way I felt before."

"Mother, you were just a little stressed trying to keep it all together. I know. I feel the same having to deal with Norm and the kids all the time."

"Rosebud, I know you mean well, but that isn't the way I want to live anymore."

"Really, Mother? Because Gloria has convinced you that you have seen the psychedelic light, or something?"

"No, dear, it was a lot more than that. After I sat and talked with your father last night, it suddenly stuck me:

I could make the decision as to whether or not I wanted to feel at peace with him."

"You're just being sentimental, Mother. And you are being far too kind after all he did to you."

"Oh, Rosemary, can't you understand? I did more harm to myself than he ever did. And, as we all now know, I was no saint as much as I wanted everyone to think otherwise. The simple fact is that I could never face the real truth before."

She couldn't. She had lied to herself—and everyone else—for so long that it had all become the way she wanted to remember it. When Gloria had told her to get honest with herself, it had jarred her. She had had an affair, and it wasn't something that "just happened." She had made it happen. She had grown so resentful about all the time Jake was spending away from her that she just wanted to do something that would bring him back to her.

Warren, Jake's business partner, seemed like the ideal choice. He was a vapid little man who spent his days in Jake's shadow. She didn't want to be with him— she just wanted to use him to get to Jake.

Of course, she didn't think of it like that back then. She had rationalized it to the point that it was more of a tragic romance—a young and unhappy woman trying desperately to find some way of winning her husband back. Jake would find out about it—she would make sure he did—and he would realize that he was losing her. Then he would do everything to win her back and never leave her lonely again.

It didn't turn out like that. All she succeeded in doing was hurting Jake and making a total mess of her own life—and her children's. She had never intended it to go as far as it did, and after she and Warren had slept together a few times, he went to Jake and confessed. Jake was furious, but at Gloria's insistence had tried to get past it. He couldn't, and C.C.'s arrival was the ever-present daily reminder that he had been cuckolded.

"And why now?"

"Because now we are at the end, Rosebud, and all of our quarrels and strife matter so little anymore. It doesn't matter who was right and who was wrong. He is about to die. He is your father, Rosebud—and John-nie's—and I now realise that I will always love him for that."

She paused to gauge her daughter's reaction before deciding to tell her more. "When I realized that, it made me unbearably sad, and after we talked I sat alone on the deck and cried like . . . well, like I haven't cried since he left."

"Oh, mother, why didn't you come to get me?"

"Because I had to be alone, dear. I had to sit there and finally admit to myself that I had driven him away— from you and Johnnie as well as from me. He told me he regretted not staying and putting up more of a fight, but it wouldn't have mattered. He couldn't love me the way I wanted to be loved, and I was too proud and insecure to let him love me the only way he could."

"It wasn't all your fault." Buddy lowered her cup and leaned forward into her mother's arms. Mary held her for a while. Buddy had always been the affectionate one.

"I agree, just like what happened last night was not all your fault."

"Really? Then whose fault was it?"

"Mine."

Buddy sat back and looked like she was trying to find something to say. Mary saved her the bother. "It is okay, Rosebud, I have to face up to all the stupid, selfish things I have done. We all do."

"What did Gloria put in that pipe?"

Buddy was trying to lighten the mood, but she had tears rolling down her cheeks. And her mother's words were lingering inside of her. Mary knew her well enough to know that.

"Laugh at me if you must, but when I had my first few puffs, I felt like I was standing outside of myself looking in and I didn't like what I saw."

"That's just paranoia, Mother. Everybody gets like that once in a while when they smoke up."

"Gloria was telling me that pot was sacred to the First Peoples, and she said that getting paranoid was just your spirit guide letting you know when you are out of kilter with yourself."

"Gloria is addled—and you will be, too, if you keep getting high with her."

"Rosebud, when a woman gets older, she has to come to terms with certain things. All that we once were begins to fade away: looks, youth—all the things that we thought were us. Then we have to face what is left. Many of us struggle to manage that change with grace and poise."

"Grace and poise? Are you high right now?"

"No, I'm not. And I can understand your reaction, but you have to believe me; this weekend has forced me to come to terms with so much."

"I still don't think it was right for Gloria to put you through all of this."

"That's what I said to her when I found out that Jake was coming."

"And what did she say?"

"Something about how I would make it worse if I was on my own."

"Typical Gloria."

Buddy meant it meanly, but Mary just smiled. True: Gloria had poked and prodded her every step of the way—and she seemed to enjoy doing some of it. A part of Mary resented her for that, but another part was grateful. Gloria had, in her own way, always tried to do what she thought was right. Mary could see that now. Gloria just wanted Mary to come to terms with Jake while there was still time. She also added that she could understand if Mary might still need to feel like a victim from time to time, but she couldn't go on blaming Jake anymore. And, having seen him the way he was, Mary understood exactly why Gloria needed to tell her all of that.

"You know you will have to face the others—and apologise to your sister."

"That's not going to change anything."

"Not immediately, but it will."

"She said I was becoming just like you."

"That girl always had a knack for using the truth to her advantage."

"So, you think she's right?"

"Rosebud: all mothers are shaped by their experiences with their own mothers—for better or worse. And I know I have not been a very good example in things like this, but please try not to repeat the mistakes I made."

"They weren't all mistakes."

"You're right, but I never could bring myself to admit to the ones that were. You see, my dear, your poor mother was riddled with shame. And believe me, I have condemned myself far more than anyone else ever could."

"You know that I never . . ."

"I know, Rosebud. I know." She paused to listen as voices emerged from the boathouse. The children were awake. "Now let's get back."

"You go get the kids, and I'll face the others."

"Are you sure, dear?"

"Yes. Just delay the kids for as long as you can."

Chapter 12

"**D**id you manage to get any sleep?" Carol asked as Heather cautiously made her way down the stairs. Heather nodded and smiled, so Carol smiled back. She could see that Heather hadn't slept much either. And she had been crying, even though she was young enough to rinse most of it away. Carol wanted to reach out and do whatever she could to comfort her. Instead, she just touched the back of the young woman's hand. "Come and sit and I will make some tea."

"I can do it, if you can show me where everything is."

"Sure," Carol agreed. "Follow me."

She led her past the main room where Norm and Johnnie were sitting at the table. Norm had been talking about how he was going to handle Buddy when she got back, and it was obvious that he had no idea what he was going to do. He'd say one thing and gauge their reactions. Then he'd say the opposite and watch them again. "Do whatever you think is right," Carol had advised him, and Norm nodded and turned for Johnnie's reaction, but he just shrugged.

Johnnie wasn't as distant this morning but still seemed reluctant to get involved. He had told Carol he just needed to get a few coffees into him and then he'd face the day. Carol had left it at that. She had wanted to tell him to go out and sit on the veranda with his father, but she held off. He would when he was ready. Besides, Jake was snoozing, and Gloria was there watching over him. Her face was tired and sad, and yet she looked so beautiful. She looked like someone who had finally gotten to put down all that had been weighing on her for years. She chased the flies from around her sleeping son's face and let him sleep, probably just as he had done at the beginning. Carol could never see herself being so serene about such a thing. It was one of the things that she never allowed herself to even think about: burying a child. The very thought of it made her shiver.

"How's C.C.?" she asked after Heather had poured her tea and perched on one of the stools by the counter. It was the center-piece of Gloria's tastefully remodeled kitchen. It was made from an old maple that Gloria had loved. It had come down after an ice storm. Gloria was upset, so Johnnie had made it in secret and installed it while Gloria was away visiting friends. He still buffed it with his sleeve every time he passed it.

"She says she is doing okay. She went for a walk and asked to be left alone for a while. I wanted to go with her, but . . . you don't think anything will happen to her?"

"Happen? No. C.C. has her own way of dealing things. She'll be fine; it's Buddy who should be worried about things 'happening.'"

"C.C. wouldn't . . .?"

"Probably not, but if I was Buddy I would take both canoes over to the island until everyone goes home."

"You're joking, right?"

"I guess so. Besides, you've nothing to worry about. C.C. has always been more than a match for her sister."

"She's not that hard inside."

Carol stopped herself from saying something flippant. "I know, but she likes to pretend she is, and we all go along with it. It's always been like that."

"She is different with me."

Carol might have scoffed a little. C.C. could be whatever her latest partner needed her to be—but only for a while. She and Heather were still at that stage.

"She was at first," Heather continued as her eyes grew bigger and softer. "She always had to be in control of everything, but this weekend has changed that. We sat and talked most of the night."

"And how was she about . . . you know."

"She was devastated, of course; for a while. Then she realized that that was the problem all along: it wasn't that her father disliked her; she just wasn't his."

"Did she actually say that?"

"Well, not in so many words. But she did seem more at ease with it all. But then I got tired and she came down to get a drink. I think she might have been talking with her . . . Jake."

"Really?" Carol tried to sound only mildly interested, but she did shoot a glance at Johnnie, who had followed them in and stood in the doorway behind Heather, just listening.

"I asked her if she was okay when she came back up. She said she was, but that she needed to walk in the woods for a while—to clear her head."

"Did she say where?" Johnnie interrupted, and his urgency unsettled Heather.

"No," she answered, and her voice wavered. "Should I go looking for her?"

"No."

Johnnie was trying to sound calm, but Carol could see through it. "Maybe," she added in Johnnie's direction, as casually as she could. "You could go and check on her."

"You don't think . . ." Heather started but seemed reluctant to finish.

"No. She just might need one of her big brother's famous pep talks."

"Yes," Heather turned her smile on Johnnie. "She told me about them."

≈

When Buddy made her way back to the cottage, Gloria was still on the veranda with Jake. She looked over as Buddy climbed the steps and smiled a strange, sad smile. Buddy tried to smile back, but she couldn't look her grandmother in the eye. She had let her down: they'd all been worried that Mary would turn Gloria's great reconciliation into a farce—boy, were they all wrong.

Gloria would forgive her, but only after they had a good talk. She would insist on holding Buddy and softly caressing her hair. She would remind her of all those other times they had curled up together—stretching back to when Buddy was a child. Buddy would just listen as the old woman's love filled her with warmth and enough encouragement to go back out and face the world—just like she did with her own kids.

Carol would forgive her too; Buddy wouldn't even have to ask. Carol was like a sister without all the baggage that siblings carried. She always seemed to know what Buddy was going through, and while they didn't always agree, Carol was always there for her.

She had seen Buddy approach, and she and Heather had slipped out the back and headed over to the dock. Buddy was grateful for that; she wasn't ready to explain herself to everyone just yet. She had to make things right with her husband first.

A lot of what had been building up inside of her had more to do with him, anyway. She had been very pushy lately and she had pushed him too far. When he walked away from her by the cottage door, she knew that he had enough of her. She knew it when they were all sitting around the fire and she knew that he was getting ready to have it out with her. She should have just shut her mouth . . . but she didn't.

When she got to the door, he was sitting alone by the table. He was staring out at the lake and his face was calm. She hadn't seen him look like that since . . . probably before the kids.

She had to admit it: she had never really been fair with him. Adapting to family life had always been a struggle for him. Back in high school, he'd always been the fun guy who never took things too seriously, and she used to like that about him. He was the one who was always telling her to chill out, but in a way, that made her feel like he really cared what happened to her.

After they had known each other long enough, she asked him if he really did. He had gotten all clumsy and tried to clown around, but when she asked again he admitted it—only, not in so many words. He said something about being really "into" her even though she got so uptight about a lot of things. He said he got it, that dealing with her parents must have been "so heavy." He also said that he'd always be there for her—to keep things "light."

She stood outside the screen door for a moment and tried to compose herself. "I am sorry," she finally offered, not sure if she should go in or wait. Norm turned slowly, like he had been woken from a dream, and his face changed at the very sight of her.

"Is there any way you can forgive me?" she asked when he didn't answer. He seemed to be thinking about it, and it seemed like he was taking forever.

"Norm, please?"

"I don't think I am the one you need to be saying sorry to."

"I know. I know." She opened the door and sidled into the room. He didn't move, so she approached him slowly and raised her arms in the hopes that he might stand up and hold her. He didn't; he just sat there and shook his head in disbelief.

"What the hell got into you?"

She tried to reach out and touch his shoulder, but he turned from her.

"I mean it, Buddy. What the hell were you thinking of?"

"Please, Norm. Don't make me go through it all again—it's bad enough. Can't we just talk first, and then I will go and face the others? And I will apologise to C.C. in front of everybody."

"Are you hoping that is going to make everything all right?"

"No, but I am still going to do it. But first, I need to say sorry to you."

"For what?"

"Everything."

She meant it. When she had snapped and told C.C. that she wasn't Jake's, she could almost feel herself falling through the last few safety nets. But who was she kidding? It was inevitable. It had been a long, slow process that she had denied for years. She had to: to admit it would have meant re-evaluating everything that she had been taught. It would have meant facing life without the comfort of all the self-righteous indignation she had inherited from her mother. It would have meant admitting that they had both been wrong about so many things.

It really began to come apart when Mary and Gloria made their pact and greeted Jake with civility. Buddy had felt the ground shift beneath her. Buddy had been all prepared to join in with her mother and stand as sullen reminders of all the terrible things Jake had done to them all.

Norm had never liked that side of her and always said that she was at her worst right after she had spent some time with her mother. He used to call it "spending time back in the coven." He said that it brought out all her negativity and turned her into a ticking time bomb just waiting to blow up over nothing. He was right about that. Normally she took it out on him, but last night she didn't. She knew he was trying to force a showdown in front of the others, so she didn't: she did something far worse.

Not that he ever really deserved her crap, anyway. When they first started going out, he had always been happy just to see her, except when she was upset—like after she'd had a row with her mother or her sister. Then he'd get so concerned and listen as she told him everything that had happened. He'd always take her side, but he never said anything against her mother and sister. He'd just hold her in his arms and let her talk, or cry, herself out. He'd hold her for ages—until he'd start to get turned on.

She used to get mad at him for that, but he'd act all innocent and say he couldn't help it. Then he'd smile and they both knew: she was turned on too, but she would never admit it. She'd even try getting all huffy and say that he was trying to take advantage of her, but he'd just wrap his arms around her again and hold her for a while. Sometimes she invented problems at home just so he'd hold her, and when they had been together long enough, she'd let him feel her up—through her clothes. That was how they had sex the first time. It should have been a shining memory, but afterwards she just felt guilty about the way she manipulated him.

"Yes, I am sorry for everything. Is there any way . . .?"

She knew that once they'd had sex, he would never leave her. That's the kind of guy he was. It should have been something good, only she took advantage of it and all the clumsy ways he showed his love and used it against him. Sure, he was still very immature and for the longest time wanted to behave like a kid, but she could always get him to do anything she wanted. That should have been a good thing, but it also became a problem. In time she started to lose respect for him. They both knew it, and he had no idea how to handle it. He'd alternate from acting out to pleading with her.

She had taken advantage of that too and made him grovel sometimes—especially in front of her family. She wanted them to know that what had happened to their mother would never happen to her. He understood that too and put up with it—most of the time.

"Do you really want to have this out right now? Why don't we just get the kids and get out of here and deal with all of this at home?"

She wasn't sure if he wanted to leave to save her any more embarrassment, or if things were going to get far worse when they were alone. "Because I need to know that I haven't lost you."

He thought about his answer for a while, and she could almost feel what was churning around inside of him. When C.C. had said to her that she was turning into her mother, Norm's face had frozen in shock. It was like hearing someone else say it made it true—and not something he had been imagining.

"Have I?" she asked when the waiting became too much.

"I don't know."

"Norm, talk to me please. Say whatever it is you have to say, just please say something."

He looked at her the way he did all those other times when he knew he was walking into one of her traps. It was a resigned look like he couldn't think of any other way of moving things forward. There wasn't: she would never forgive him until she felt she had power over him again.

"What do you want me to say?"

"I want you to tell me what you are feeling." Buddy began to sob and raised her arms toward him again. "I want you to tell me that you can't stand watching me become just like my mother."

He stepped back from her, but she caught hold of his forearms. He could have shaken her off, but he didn't. He just stood with his arms extended and waited.

"I need you to tell me how frustrating it has been putting up with me. I need you to tell me that I have to change or you will leave me." She was crying uncontrollably but still he stood back. "And I need you to tell me that I have to be different from now on."

He let her hold his arms for a little while as he seemed to be searching for the right words, but he didn't find them. Slowly, he withdrew and turned and walked away.

≈

C.C. walked and walked with no real direction in mind. It didn't matter; she knew the woods and she just needed time alone. She kept telling herself that it all made sense now: all those years of feeling different; all those years of trying to fit in and conform to what she had been told was normal. Nothing was normal. Everything was just a contrived consensus of what was socially acceptable. She had been coming to that realization for the last few years and once again it was crystalized.

It had begun when she first got together with Michelle. That was when she had finally gotten honest with herself about her sexuality—even if a part of her was just acting rebelliously. She had been going through the motions with the men she had dated, and it always felt like that. Buddy used to say that she lacked the patience and caring that a real relationship demanded. She even went on and on about how much she and Norm had to adjust.

C.C. didn't buy any of that, and while the first time she made love with Michelle felt strange and awkward, she blew past it with her usual bravado and afterwards it just felt right.

Still, deep down she was worried about what her family might think, but she dealt with that as she dealt with all the other issues she had with them: she just confronted them and forced them to accept her. Her mother had tried to make it all about her—as if it was another one of the trials and tribulations life had prepared just for her.

Johnnie and Carol took it all in stride as she expected them to, knowing that Johnnie only ever wanted his little sister to find what was right for her. Carol too, only in a different way.

Buddy said she was happy about it, but C.C. could see right through that. Buddy claimed that her only concern was Mary's reaction, but that wasn't true. Buddy always said that she just wanted them to be in a place where everyone could be happy. That was why she had lashed out the way she did: she was getting frustrated just like she always did, and this time she had gone too far.

Now it was up to C.C. to decide how she would react to that. The others would be expecting the worst, and the vindictive side of her wanted to oblige.

The woods were bright and splendid in their colors and, despite everything, C.C. couldn't help but feel happy. The end of summer had always been the time when she regathered what she would have to be to go back and face the world. She had never lacked confidence and always butted her way through whatever life put before her, but she was beginning to count the costs of that.

Michelle's leaving had been hard. Once, on the very same spot overlooking the lake, C.C. had defined her renewed self as a part of that relationship. She had decided that she and Michelle would be strong together and defy anyone who would try to judge them. And when she felt herself wavering, she thought she could rely on Michelle's strength. She was almost ten years older than C.C. and didn't take shit from anybody.

Things would have to be different with Heather. She had strength too, but it was a softer, gentler kind. C.C. had been mistaken about that; she had thought that Heather was just someone she could get over Michelle with. It wasn't like she set out to use Heather, but stuff like that happened all the time. Before the weekend, she had felt a few pangs of guilt about that.

That was one of the things with Michelle; C.C. had never felt comfortable exposing her doubts or uncertainties. Michelle had no time for things like that, so C.C. had behaved that way too.

It paid off at work where she earned the reputation for being someone who just got things done. Some people didn't like her for that, but they still had to kiss her ass. Her bosses loved her and showered her with all the perks and promotions that results like hers earned.

Still, when she was alone and thought about things, she often felt more like a fraud. In her worst moments she felt like a poor little unwanted girl with so many issues.

Some people at work called her a ball-crusher and while she loved hearing that, it wasn't really her: it was the way life had made her. When she was really honest with herself she could admit it: she was angry, and everyone was going to pay for the way her father had treated her.

Michelle knew and always encouraged that side of her. In fact, their relationship often felt that it was as much about in-your-face activism as it was about two people in love. C.C. had ignored that until it was too late.

Michelle was always going on about breaking rules and throwing out all the old values that "straight" society had imposed. "Marriage and monogamy are just concepts," she often railed. "Two people should only be together because they love each other—and only while they love each other."

C.C. had found that unsettling at first, but she soon realised that behind her façade Michelle was just like her—brazen and blustery. And just like her, Michelle always had to seem in control.

It all fell apart after what happened in Chicago.

C.C. had been there for a conference and had a little too much to drink. She ended up in bed with a couple of sales reps from Dallas—a man and a woman. It didn't mean anything; it was just one of those things that happened when she drank too much—and popped a few pills. They had been at a bar all night, and when the other woman had suggested it, C.C. couldn't back down.

Michelle couldn't see it that way and left. C.C. tried pleading, reminding Michelle of all the things she had said about stuff like that, but Michelle didn't want to know. She said that C.C. lacked the ability to love. She even said that she doubted if C.C. ever could.

Those words still stung, and if she was to try to have a real relationship with Heather, it would have to be about real commitment, and she was finally ready for that. She had spent her whole life reacting to something that wasn't the way it had always seemed. There were still all kinds of issues to deal with, but many of them weren't hers. She'd still have to deal with them, but from now on, it would be more about healing. She and Heather had sat up talking, and Heather had said that she was good with all of that. She said that she wanted their relationship to be the warm, comforting place where they could regenerate and renew themselves.

Before the weekend, C.C. would have found that far too girly, but things had changed.

≈

"Are you okay?"

C.C. turned slowly, reluctant to re-emerge from the quiet space she had found for herself. Susie was standing at the edge of the trees and seemed concerned and reluctant to encroach any further. C.C. was standing far closer to the edge of the cliff than she had realized. It was only twenty feet high, but probably seemed far higher to the kid.

"Sure. Why?"

"I dunno. It just looked like you might be thinking of jumping."

"Yeah, I just might. But let me ask you something: why are you out here?"

"Everybody is looking for you. I just figured this is where you would be."

"And you thought I came here to end everything?"

"I dunno. Maybe."

"Oh, Susie, things are not that bad. I just like to come up here when I have to sort stuff out."

Susie didn't say anything, but she didn't look convinced—in fact, she looked a bit like Gloria did when C.C. was trying to bullshit her way through something. It was one of the things Mary and Buddy often found unnerving about the kid, but C.C. liked her. Susie was like Johnnie and Gloria all rolled into one—with a lot of Carol thrown in.

"Do you ever come up here?" she asked and beckoned Susie loser to the edge. "Your dad used to bring me up here when I was little. He always said that one day he would throw me over."

"Did he?"

"Nay, he just waited until I had the courage to jump by myself."

"Yeah, sounds like something he would do."

C.C. paused to look closely at her niece. She had walked right to the edge and was looking down into the deep, cool water below. "Has anyone ever told you that you look a lot like Gigi?"

Susie turned slowly and smiled. "Mum and Dad always say that you look just like her."

"Oh, my God, do I look that old already?"

"I don't think that was what they meant."

"I dunno. With this family, you never can tell." She meant it as a joke, but Susie was looking a bit concerned again. "Hey," C.C. asked to change the mood. "Want to jump in with me?"

"Really? It looks a bit too high."

"Do you really think that I would ask you to do something that might hurt you?"

"I dunno. Like you said, with this family . . ." But she was already peeling off her shirt and shorts. She always wore her bathing suit underneath.

"Okay," C.C. agreed and began to take her clothes off. "Let's do this."

When they were ready, they reached out to touch each other's hands and jumped forward. Susie managed to turn her body in the air and plunged in arms first. C.C. wasn't so coordinated and landed firmly on her ass.

"Oh my God," Susie shrieked as she broke the surface and brushed the water from her face. "Let's do that again."

"Sure," C.C. agreed as she reached down to rub her burning ass. "Just give me a minute."

The climb back up was far more difficult than C.C. remembered, but Susie didn't seem to have a problem, even stopping a few times to lend her aunt a helping hand.

"That was the most fun," Susie laughed again after they had climbed back from the third jump.

"Yeah," C.C. agreed, trying to match her niece's enthusiasm. Her ass was still burning and most of her muscles were beginning to ache. "I used to do this all the time when I was a kid. It helped."

"Did it help now . . . you know . . . with what happened?"

"Let me ask you something. What would you do if you found out that your father wasn't your father?"

Susie got all serious for a moment—the way she did when she was trying to think like a grown-up. "I dunno. My father has always been so great; I don't think it would matter."

"Yeah, you really lucked out on the father thing, but that's my point."

Susie seemed a little upset by that, and C.C. realized it wasn't the type of thing she should be asking a teenager—even one who could seem so adult at times. "Never mind all that; I'm still just trying to sort things out in my head."

Susie nodded and reached over to touch her aunt's shoulder, like she would with a friend. "So, what are you going to do . . . you know . . . about Aunt Buddy and all?"

"Well, right after my ass stops burning, I am going to back down there and face them all. I am going to tell them all that I am fine and then I am going to walk right up to my sister. I'm going to look her straight in the eye and I'm going to tell her that I forgive her."

"Won't that be hard?"

"Are you kidding? It will almost kill me, but in this family, you gotta play smart and, after the dust has settled for a while, I am going milk this one for years."

Susie looked a bit shocked at that, and C.C. had to backtrack—the kid was still a kid. "I'm not serious, you know?"

"I dunno. It sounded like you were."

"Yeah, it did, didn't it?"

Chapter 13

"I knew I shouldn't have come."

Jake looked totally miserable and even more pale and worn out. Gloria almost felt impatient with him. "Nonsense. This is just another family squabble. It will blow over soon enough."

"And then?"

"And then we will be able to remember what was really important."

"Oh, Mother, let it go. We can't undo the past."

"That is not what I am trying to do. I just want the past to end."

"It will soon enough."

"Yes, son, you will die, but the rest of us will continue on and you will still be a part of us for as long as we live."

"Given the mess I have made, that is hardly comforting."

"Well, it should be." Gloria tried to sound authoritative, but her heart was aching—for her son and for his children. She reached out and checked his face. The day was getting warmer, so she loosened the blanket a bit. "And you shouldn't be worrying yourself about any of it. Everything will be fine in a few days."

"I hope you are right."

"I hope so too," Gloria muttered to herself. She wasn't so sure anymore. Some good would come out of it all, but the cost was going to be high. C.C. was never one to bury the hatchet, and whatever was going to happen between her and Buddy was going to test Mary. "Besides, what's done is done. Let's not spend any more time on it."

Jake smiled back at her and for a moment, he almost seemed to forget his pain and discomfort. "But I am glad we have had this time together."

"Well, I'm glad for that." She smiled back at him, but in her mind she was thinking back to when Harry had died. He should have given Jake the chance.

"He did the right thing."

"Who?"

"My father. It was better that I wasn't there at the end."

"Oh, son, let's not talk about that now."

"There will not be another time. We both know that."

"But we don't need to rehash all of that."

"Perhaps not, but I would like you to know that I understand him now. It was better that things did not end the way they would have. I was too angry with him. I would just have wanted to say things that would have hurt him. That is the difference between my children and me. They may not like me, but they don't hate me."

"Of course they don't."

"And that is to your credit—and to Mary's."

"Yours too. You were not such a bad person."

"Perhaps, but I was a terrible father."

"Your children don't seem to think so—even C.C."

He had nothing to say to that and just shrunk back down inside of his blanket. Gloria let it go at that. She could see how much the effort to talk was taking from him. How was he ever going to make the trip back?

≈

After C.C. showed up with Susie and the great "search party" had been called off, Carol tried to organize lunch. Everybody was anxious to start heading back, but they had to eat first—it would be four to five hours back to Toronto, depending on traffic. She was hoping to get some help, but perhaps it was better that they were all off doing their own thing.

Besides, it was more a matter of picking through all that was in the fridge. Some things, like the salads, Gloria would get around to eating, but the chicken had to be finished—and the left over burgers and hot dogs. It wasn't going to be pretty, but nobody was expecting too much.

"Eating the leftovers was all part of the cottage experience," Mary always said when she used to prepare it. She was outside on the veranda with Jake and Gloria, sitting there like all that had happened long ago, all that had twisted her and dominated every day since, had never really been.

When she had first started to act differently, Carol didn't buy it but kept her opinions to herself. She couldn't help but feel that Mary was acting like a kid trying to turn over a new leaf—all in one day. Instead, Carol had just watched and waited. Deep down, she hoped it was for real this time—for everybody's sake, but it was so hard to know with Mary anymore.

Normally, Carol and Johnnie would have talked about it, but this wasn't a normal weekend. He seemed to be finally coming out of whatever funk he'd been in. It had to be more than his dad dying—it had to be.

Still, it did seem to be what had gotten to Mary. And it didn't really matter if some of it was superficial. Anything would be better than the way she was, for her own sake too.

Carol stood for a moment and looked at them all. Gloria was smiling a sad, resigned, kind of smile. It was like she was happy to accept that this was as good as it could possibly get—given the circumstances. Carol's heart went out to her, and she almost wanted to follow and take the old woman in her arms. But in that moment, they all turned to look at the kids. Susie and Joey were keeping the little ones distracted, and it had turned into a pile on. Even Susie was in the middle of it. Jake, Mary, and Gloria watched for a while until Gloria made a comment that made them all laugh. Carol wouldn't have to worry about her; Gloria knew how to look after herself.

The same could not be said for Jake. By the looks of him, he would be dead in days. Hopefully he wouldn't do it in the car on the way back to the airport.

Carol almost chided herself for thinking that, but she was far too pragmatic. At the end of the day, she owed Jake nothing and while she could respect that he was Johnnie's father, he had made enough ripples in all their lives. She didn't wish him harm and she hoped he passed peacefully as long as it was somewhere else. Johnnie hadn't mentioned when he was dropping him off, but who else was going to do it?

Mary would be fine, too, even if her reformation were to start wearing thin. She would move in with Buddy and . . . or would she? Things between Buddy and Norm were going to take some mending, and even Mary would have to realize that.

Carol did think about it briefly, but no—there was no way Mary could come and live with them. It just wouldn't be fair on any of them.

She turned from the window, still thinking about that when Norm poked his head around the door. He had an empty beer bottle in his hand and was headed for the fridge.

"Just the man I wanted to talk with."

"Really?"

"Yeah—why does that surprise you?"

"I dunno. It just feels like everyone is avoiding me this morning."

"And you have no idea why?"

"I guess, but I didn't have anything to do with it."

"Not yet."

"What do you mean?"

"Oh, Norm, don't try to be coy—you're too transparent."

He shuffled a bit and looked so uncomfortable that Carol had to cut him a break. "But don't worry; you make it seem cute."

"Don't tell me—tell the others."

"Maybe I will. So, have you decided what you are going to do?"

"What do you mean?"

She thought about looking at him with total exasperation, but Buddy had probably worn that one out. "What are you going to do about Buddy?"

"I dunno. What do you think I should do?"

"I think," Carol answered slowly as she walked to the kitchen table and picked up the big carving knife. "That you should start talking, or I will be forced to cut it out of you."

"Yeah, like you ever would."

"Norm, after the weekend we have all been through, do you really want to test me?" She waved the knife at him, but she couldn't help but smile. "Get your ass over here"—she pointed to the stool by the counter—"and start talking."

Norm thought about it for a moment, shrugged, walked to the fridge and took out a beer. He scratched his stubble with the cap and finally sat. It was like the way Joey used to get when he wanted to seem defiant but didn't want to risk too much escalation. Carol watched him until he sat and opened the beer.

"Do you really think having a few beers right now is such a good idea?"

"Yeah, I do, actually, and from now on, everyone's gonna have to deal with a whole different me."

"Really?"

"Yeah. No more Mr. Nice Guy who takes all the shit. I'm done with all that, Carol. I'm done with been picked at. It's time I put some of myself back into my life."

"And a lot of beer," Carol nodded towards the half-empty bottle. Norm was really chugging it down—something he only did when he was trying to get wasted.

"So what? I'm at the goddamn cottage, for Christ's sake. A guy's supposed to be able to chill at the cottage."

"How many have you had?"

"Not enough."

"You know you are going to have to drive soon, and the cops will be everywhere."

"Do I, Carol? Do I really have to?"

"No, I suppose you don't. Only, you know that Buddy is going to make a fuss if you ask her to. She hates driving in traffic."

Norm gulped the rest of his beer and headed back towards the fridge for another. Carol thought about getting in his way, but this wasn't her fight. She was trying to calm things down.

"I'm gonna let you in on a little secret." Norm grinned and took a long swig of the new beer. "Driving in traffic is no piece of cake for me, either—only before, I just did it. Not anymore, Carol. Things have changed. Besides," he added, as if his announcement didn't hold enough weight. "Buddy's going to get pissed about traffic whether she's driving or I am. This way, she can deal with it while I sit back and enjoy a bit of a buzz. It's going to be my new take on life—screw it all and have another beer."

"You should think about getting hats and t-shirts made, and hold meetings," Carol said without looking up. "Listen, Norm. I get it. I really do. Only, this isn't you."

"It's the new me."

"Norm, you are still going to have to work things out—one way or the other."

"What's that mean?"

"Either you are going to pack up and end things with Buddy, or you are going to try and work things out. Right?"

"Maybe."

"Do you see any other option?"

"I dunno. I guess I haven't thought that far ahead."

"Norm! Don't be an asshole about it. What do you really want to happen?"

"I dunno. I guess I don't want to end it all. I just want things to be different."

"And . . . ?"

"I dunno."

"Oh, for Christ's sake, Norm. What is the one thing you would ask Buddy to change if she was standing here?"

He seemed a little surprised at Carol's outburst but stopped to think for a moment. "I guess, more than any-thing . . . I just wish she could see me as the person I really am again—and not as she thinks I should be . . . you know, as some fairy-tale image of what a husband or a father should be."

≈

"Yeah, I can get past it," C.C. said in her most matter-of-fact voice. She was sitting on the dock with her mother. Gloria had sent Mary over to make sure everything was all right with C.C. while making sure that the others gave them time and space to sort things out. "And as everyone else seems to have found Jesus this weekend, I am sure I'll get around to forgiving her someday."

"That is good," Mary answered so softly as if she was afraid of upsetting the delicate balance. Before, C.C. would have been ready to fly off the handle when it suited her, but today she was willing to cut her mother some slack.

"And will you ever be able to forgive your mother?"

C.C. turned and looked out across the lake. There were so many times when her mother had acted so sanctimoniously, berating her for every little thing she did. Like those times when she had stayed out late with boys, or when she had first gotten together with Michelle—so many things that had stuck inside of her and burned like ulcers. But now, they mattered less. Her mother was a flawed and frail human being, and C.C. had always known that. She was tempted to mention that—that she was the one who had been right all along, but what was the point? She'd just end up carrying all the same old crap around instead of letting it all go, once and for all.

"Yes, Mother, I can do that. I got some sorting out to do, but I can do that. But there is one thing you are going to have to do for me. You are going to have to be for real this time." She paused and watched her mother's face contort. She wasn't trying to be cruel. It was just that they had all been down this road so many times before.

"So, it is conditional."

"Yeah, I guess it is—but, then again, everything is when you really think about it."

"And will it be conditional with your sister too?"

"Look, Mother," C.C. started like she was trying to explain something she didn't yet understand. "We have all been affected by the . . . shadows of the past, but it is all out in the open now. And that's a good thing. Now, we just have to wait and see what each one of us does with it."

Mary nodded and smiled before hauling herself up. She was on the verge of tears, but she kept them inside. "Thank you, C.C. Thank you for giving us another chance."

"No problem," C.C. smiled back, trying so hard to keep her own emotions in check. "You're still, and always have been, my mother."

"Thank you." Mary turned and walked a few steps back towards the cottage. Then she turned slowly and looked back. "You know, if there is one single thing we should all take from this weekend, it is this: it is so easy to rationalize our own mistakes and just as easy to make too big a deal of the mistakes of others."

And that was it. She turned back and walked away. C.C. had to smile. Even with her dignity in shreds around her ankles, her mother could be a total pain in the ass—effortlessly.

She was still smiling at that when Johnnie sat down beside her.

"Yo, bro, what's cooking?"

"Yeah, fine. You doing okay?"

"Peachy."

"Great. Listen, there is something I got to tell you."

"Not another goddamn family secret."

"No . . . well . . . kind of. It's about da . . . my father."

"How many secrets does that man have?"

"Just one more."

≈

From the corner of her eye, Gloria could see Buddy make her way around the other side of the veranda. She still wasn't ready to face them all together. Gloria understood and rose to follow her. Jake looked up like he didn't want to be left alone, but Mary was heading back, and she could sit with him for a while.

When Gloria rounded the corner of the cottage, Buddy was standing beneath the kitchen window listening to Carol and Norm talk.

"Now, Rosebud, you know better than to be listening in like that. You never hear anything good."

Buddy looked sheepish, but she also looked like she was about to cry.

"Come." Gloria offered her arm. "Let's you and I stroll until lunch is ready."

Buddy didn't hesitate and snuggled in besides her, almost making it difficult to walk, but Gloria didn't mind. It felt good. "Well, my dear. How are you managing?"

"You mean after ruining everybody's weekend?"

"Oh, don't be silly. You were just a side show in this great circus of a family."

"That's the story of my life: even when I do something outlandish, I am still a side show."

"My dear little Rosebud, that sounds far too much like self-pity. It may seem warm and comforting at first, but I have found that it is not unlike peeing in your pants. It is, ultimately, embarrassing."

Buddy almost laughed at that. "You do say the oddest things."

"Of course I do. I am old, and I smoke pot. How else would you expect me to behave?"

"Oh, I don't know. I don't know anything anymore. I thought I did, but . . ."

"My dear, the only real advantage of getting old is that you realize that you don't have to know everything. In fact, you come to realize how little you do know, and that becomes a great comfort in the end."

"But what about all the things we have to deal with? How are we supposed to know what is right or wrong?"

"Oh, I think we always know right from wrong. Only we have found it advantageous to distort them to suit our purposes from time to time."

Buddy stiffened a bit and might have pulled away, but Gloria drew her closer. "We all do it, Rosebud. There is no shame in admitting it."

"Until it costs us everything."

"I don't think that you have lost everything."

"Oh, Gloria, I love that you are always there to pick us up and help us go back out there, but even you have to admit that I may have gone too far this time."

"I'm not so sure. Yes, your sister is going to make you pay for what you did. She will say that she has forgiven you, but she will also behave like she doesn't feel she can ever trust you again. Sadly, my dear, it is how a woman claims her pound of flesh."

Buddy didn't react to that, so Gloria walked in silence for a while.

"And your husband still loves you," she casually mentioned as she motioned for them to sit overlooking the shore. "It may not seem like that, right now, but I can still see it in his eyes. He is hurt, but you know how to make things better."

"I'm not sure."

"Of course you do."

"I meant about him still loving me."

"Rosebud, don't take this the wrong way, but you didn't start being unkind to him this weekend."

"So, you think that I have been unkind to him?"

"Stop it, dear. Let's talk without the dramatics and denials."

"These are my feelings."

"Perhaps, but they are hardly the right things to steer by right now. My point is that you and your husband have been sliding down this slope for a while. I'm not saying that he is right and you are wrong. It is never that simple. What I am saying is that you didn't just get here, and getting out will take time and effort."

"If he gives me the time and effort."

"That should not be a consideration for you. If you want him, then give everything you have to getting him back—except your self-esteem. I have found that those of us who give that just become bitter anyway."

"You almost make it sound easy."

"It is not going to be easy, but you will find that there are those who will help. Your brother and Carol will always be there for you no matter what. And even your mother and your sister, but you might do better to avoid them for a while.

"And to that point," Gloria continued as she looked across the lake. "I want you to know that I have asked your mother to stay with me for a while. It will help me deal with . . . Jake."

"But mother is coming to live with me. It's all been arranged."

Gloria settled herself and decided on her best approach. "Your mother and I both think that it might be better for her to stay here with me—at least for a while. I will need her here, and it will give you time to straighten things out at home."

"And did either of you stop to think that I might need her?"

"My dear, right now your own family must come first, over all of us. You must go home and try to make things right again. And not just for you and Norm. You must make things right so that your children can continue to grow in a loving, stable environment."

That seemed to mollify Buddy for a moment, but her face clouded over again. "I just don't know what it is I have to do. I need somebody there to help me."

"Rosebud, you have the hardest job in front of you, and only you can find the right solution. Do not look to your mother—or me—on this one. We have both done so poorly in our own lives. If there is a lesson we can offer, then it should be that when you are in doubt, stop and think about how your mother or I might deal with it and do the opposite."

Buddy nearly laughed at that, so Gloria gave her a little squeeze. "A mother's role is really very simple. You just have to make everyone happy all the time."

Buddy did laugh at that, but it sounded hollow and tired.

"And by everyone," Gloria continued as encouragingly as she could, "I also mean you."

"And that's the real trick. I just have no idea how to even begin."

"Rosebud, this weekend has been about so many things that weren't right, but it must never be allowed to overshadow all the good things we are, too. And you, as much as any of us, are far more good than bad. You already have everything you will need. You have a good father to your children. You both have provided a good home for them to grow up in. You both have done so many things right—probably so many that you take them for granted. What you have to do now will not be easy, or fast, but you will be able to do it.

"And I think you will be pleasantly surprised by your husband's reaction. He is hurt right now, and angry, but when he gets past that you will see that he still loves you. And most important, he still wants to be 'in love' with you. You just have to give him every reason to move past what happened, and you will have to be patient and let him do it in his own time."

Chapter 14

"**G**irl power, girl power," C.C. chanted as she pranced into the kitchen, followed by Heather and Susie. They were dressed like the Spice Girls—something Susie used to do with her friends when they were little. Carol had to laugh even as she felt her eyebrow rise. They were all really into it, especially C.C.

"Now move your mommy-jeaned ass out of the way. We are going make this lunch a proper happening."

Carol laughed and stood back to watch them all. She had everything laid out, but if the girls wanted to take over . . .

"Sure, knock yourselves out and, if I may say so: you seem very happy with yourself."

"You mean for someone who just found out that half of their life was a lie?"

"No, I just meant in general. You're normally hungover by this stage."

"Aren't you sweet for remembering that? Anyway, the girls and I are taking over. We're going to make this a lunch to remember. And afterwards, Heather and I want to drive Susie and Joey back to the city."

"Why?"

"Well." C.C. sidled closer so she could speak softly— but still loud enough for Heather to hear. "I thought it might be good for you and Johnnie to have some time to decompress. I think we all really got to him this weekend."

"Yeah, but why are you really taking the kids?"

"Because, silly." She leaned forward to whisper into Carol's ear. "Heather really likes being around them."

"Okay . . ." Carol was trying not to laugh: C.C. was changing her spots again. "But the person who might benefit most from your generosity would be Buddy. Take her kids; it might spare them from . . . you know."

"Sure," C.C. didn't bat an eyelid. "We'd love to. Only, we just have the four seats, and you know how Buddy can be about buckling up and stuff like that."

"No problem." Carol was enjoying herself. C.C. had to be reasonable in front of Heather, so it was as good a time as any to push her back towards her sister: Carol and Johnnie had become experts in family repairs. "You guys can ride in the truck; it's got extra seats in the cab. And Johnnie has always loved that car of yours."

"Oh, let's," Heather and Susie almost purred like cats on the prowl. Carol knew what was going on: Susie had developed some expertise of her own.

"Yeah, let's," C.C. agreed without a flinch but took a moment to find the right face before she turned back to the others. "Oh my God, we are going to have so much fun."

"Yeah, so much fun," Carol joined in and they all did a little silly dance.

"Seriously," C.C. sidled back when they were done and hugged Carol. "This is for you and Johnnie. For everything you guys do."

"Thanks, but I'd rather you gave us your car instead."

"Sure. Take it."

"And you have to adopt our children."

"We'd love to, wouldn't we, Heather?"

Heather actually looked a bit scared, so Carol let it go at that. "Now let's get this lunch on the table—and they are not mommy jeans. See?" She raised the hem of her shirt to show. "Hipsters, actually."

"Your mum is so cool." Heather leaned across to Susie. "And so is Aunt C.C."

Carol had to look away before her heart burst. Her little girl was becoming a woman.

≈

Norm was a little thorny throughout lunch but had just about managed to keep a lid on it—probably in deference to Jake and because it was the last time they would all get to spend some time with him. Buddy knew she would pay for that later, and everything else, all the way home . . . and beyond. It would be better if the kids didn't have to sit through that just now. Later, when they were back in their own house, she could find all kinds of ways to distract them from the worst of it.

She tried not to think about it and focused on her father instead. Gloria had asked them all to try to be as natural as they could, and it was a strain—even Jake seemed to sense it. She almost wished that they could all just get up and say their goodbyes and go back to whatever the rest of life had in store for them, already. She knew she would feel terrible later for thinking like that—she just couldn't help it. She was feeling more lost than she had ever felt before.

Her mother seemed to know what she was thinking and smiled over at her. Buddy smiled back, but they both knew it was just reflex, so she concentrated on her father and tried to seem like she cared. That was the worst part: she didn't.

There were lots of very good reasons for that, but it still felt bad. Nothing should have mattered now that he was sitting opposite her struggling to talk, but it did. He was always that area of her life that she could never make right.

Norm used to tell her that was a big part of her problem. He said it wasn't her job to "make things right." She liked when he told her stuff like that, even if it went in one ear . . . but she liked it.

She wanted to look over at him, but she was afraid of how he might react. She would prefer to deal with his scorn and his sullenness when they were at home—in private. Now she just wanted them all to feel like a family for a little while longer.

"Daddy, Daddy," Dwayne and Brad came charging over from the kids table. "Guess what? We're going to go home in Uncle Johnnie's truck."

"With Susie and Joey. C.C. will be driving." Carol ventured after Norm had said nothing.

"I don't think so." He finally announced like a verdict.

"Ah, Dad. Can we please?"

"No."

"Oh, let them," Gloria offered instinctively but kept her head down. It might have been to avoid causing provocation, or she might be getting ready to charge like a bull. Her voice was calm but her eyes flashed.

"No. They are going to ride with me and their mother."

That set off the cacophony, starting with the kids going into their rehearsed tantrums, Mary and Gloria rushing to placate them, and Jake wheezing like he might explode. Buddy knew there was nothing she could say or do, so she just sat back. Norm was right all those times he complained that her family never took him seriously. And this time was no different: no one was going to accept his decision.

Normally, he would have vacillated until Johnnie found him some way out, but Johnnie showed no signs of wanting to get involved in this one. Norm looked around at each face in turn like he was trapped.

"You know what!" He stood up suddenly and slammed his two hands on the picnic table, causing everything on it to wobble and shake. It got everybody's attention, and they all fell silent and stared at him. That seemed to un-nerve him a little and he grew flustered—Buddy could always tell.

"I've had it with this family," he finally blurted out and turned and walked from the table muttering "piss and shit" almost every other word.

Carol was to first to react and got up to follow him, but C.C. held her back. "I got this one. You don't mind, Buddy?"

Buddy just shook her head and tried not to cry. Now, instead of being able to remember her last time with her father . . .

≈

"Slow down," C.C. called after him when they were almost at the dock. "These shoes . . ."

"Oh, great," Norm exploded as he turned around and glared at her. "What the hell are you here for? Are you hoping to be able to go back and tell Buddy that we made out, or something?"

"Cool it, Norm. I get it. And you have every right to be pissed . . . at Buddy."

"I'm pissed at all of you."

"Even Johnnie and Carol?"

"Them, not so much."

C.C. could always get him talking. "And the kids?"

"Nay, not the kids either."

"Heather? Gloria?"

"Nay."

"Jake?"

"Kind of, but he has enough on his plate."

"So, it's basically me, Buddy, and probably my mom."

"Mary's not so bad."

"But definitely me and Buddy."

"Yeah, no. It's the whole goddamn thing, C.C. It's all so messed up."

"Yeah," C.C. agreed and got a little closer to him. "Always has been, only before I didn't have a goddamn clue why." She was hoping to play vulnerable—that always got to him. "But I guess now that's it all out there, you're probably wishing to hell that you never got mixed up with any of us."

"That thought has crossed my mind so many times it feels like a goddamn TV commercial."

"Yeah, I hear you, bro. Listen, I know where there's a few cold brewskis. Want to split a couple before we ride off into the sunset?"

He said nothing, so she fetched the beers and brought them back, walking towards him like she was in a beer commercial. That got to him, and he was starting to thaw out.

"Did I ever tell you that I used to have a crush on you?" She leaned in, but she got too close.

"Ah shit, C.C. Is this how you plan to get even with Buddy?"

Damn it. She had gotten too cocky and now would have to bull her way through. She moved back a little so she could look directly into his eyes. "Yeah, no. That's not happening. What I was trying to tell you was the reason I had a crush on you was because of what Buddy used to tell me about you."

"Ah, can't you just leave it alone already?"

"Okay, Norm, I'll drop it. After I say just one more thing." She leaned in again more slowly and felt him react, despite himself. "Sometimes, the things you said to Buddy when she was down were the same things that kept me going. I never told you that before."

"So, why are you telling me now?"

"Because you are thinking of dumping Buddy."

"I haven't decided anything."

"Maybe, but you are thinking about it."

"So what if I am? You know what things have been like."

"Yeah, I do. And I wouldn't blame you if you did. It's only that the guy who used to say all those things to Buddy wouldn't give up on her when she needs him the most."

"That guy died. He was smothered to death."

"I dunno. I hope he's still around because we all need him right now."

She leaned forward and kissed his cheek. She even looked into his eyes as she drew back. He was almost there. "Hey, why don't you come back and watch while Heather and I pack up the truck?" She got up and held out her hand to him. "We might even wear our shorts. That might resuscitate part of him."

"C.C., don't start that shit again."

"What?"

"You're a right prick-teaser, you are." But he finished his beer and rose to follow.

"Yeah, I still got it. Just don't know how much I will need it anymore, though."

"Wow. Are you and Heather that serious?"

"Not yet, but we're getting there. C'mon, let's get back. I am going to need Johnnie to show me how to operate that thing."

"I could show you."

"Nay, it's a family thing and you're never going to be one of us."

"That's the plan." But he did follow her back to the others.

≈

Johnnie was clearly enjoying being behind the wheel of C.C.'s BMW—the little Barbie Car Carol and Buddy had named it one evening after they had too much wine. They weren't really jealous; they were just pissed off. They had all gotten together for dinner, and C.C. had shown up in one of her moods. It was right after Michelle, so they should have cut her a break, but Carol wasn't in the mood. C.C. was going through one of her high-maintenance periods and called Johnnie day and night and whined and cried for hours. The poor guy hardly got any sleep.

"What would you think of dumping the kids on C.C. and taking a little road trip in this little minx?" Johnnie smiled over and tried to put his elbow on the window, but the angle was all wrong. Still, it was the happiest she had seen seem since he had picked his father up.

"Sure. When?"

"Right now."

"If only, babe. If only we could."

"Why not?"

"I'm not even going to answer that, but it is nice to see you are back on the sunnier side. Care to tell me why you had your knickers in a twist the last few days?"

"Yeah, about that." He checked his side mirror and powered into the passing lane. He had to break immediately, but Carol let it pass without comment.

"Do I have to?"

"No, you can just bottle it up inside you, and the kids and I can deal with it some weekend when we bring you up here to die."

"Okay, okay. I'll tell you. My old man asked me something and I couldn't do it."

Carol was about to make a joke when she noticed the look on his face. She waited for a moment and slowly turned to look at him. He looked over and tried to smile, but he was pained.

"I see, and is it something you want to share with me?"

He nodded, but didn't say anything.

"It's okay if you want to tell me later."

"No, I'm okay telling you about it. It's just that it was pretty messed-up. He asked me to help him . . . you know . . . end it all."

They rode in silence while they both tried to figure out what to say next.

"Oh, babe, that must have been terrible."

"It was. Of course I couldn't, but . . . it really messed me up inside."

"Why didn't you talk to me about it?"

"I talked to C.C. and she made me tell Gloria."

"And what did she say?" Carol tried to sound as even as possible, but inside she was churning. Jake shouldn't have asked, and she wished Johnnie had told her first.

"She was pretty pissed at him for asking. Then she came back and said that she had sorted it out. She would have Jake picked up by ambulance and driven back to his plane. And she said it in that voice, too. You know the one."

"Yeah," Carol agreed. "Good for her." She turned away so he couldn't see her eyes grow wider. She knew exactly what Gloria was really going to do.

"Do you ever wonder if bringing the kids up here is such a great idea?"

"Wow, Johnnie, you must be really fed up with them all."

"Yeah, and can we do Christmas with your family this year?"

"We're already doing Thanksgiving, and my parents go to Florida for Christmas."

"That could be nice, too."

"Forget it. We are not going into hiding."

"I was thinking it would be more like the witness protection program."

"We could, but who is going to be there to put the pieces back together the next time your sisters go at it? Buck up, sissy-boy, it's the life of the first born."

"How come we never have to deal with stuff like this with your family?"

"That's because my entire family has a strong robotic streak. My grandmother used to say that our great-grand-father was so introverted that he had to build his own wife from parts he had around the shop—he was clock maker back in the old country. She said that it all worked out re-ally well until he wound her too tight."

"Really?"

"Of course. My point is that all families are just petri dishes for growing all kind of craziness. Yours is just that bit extra special crazy."

"And you think exposing our kids is good because ...?"

"It will help them build immunity."

"Is that even possible?"

"You're looking at proof."

"Yeah, but you're part-robot."

"And so are our kids."

"It's a much smaller part. And besides, they're part me, too."

"And what makes you think that you are their father?"

"What?"

"Just keeping a family tradition."

"Now that was low."

"Yeah, it was. Sorry. I was just goofing off. I didn't mean offence."

"None taken. It's actually pretty fitting."

"Thanks, babe, you know I still love you."

"Enough to let me be the father of your next child?"

"No way. There's more than enough crazy around my kids, already."

"Yeah, maybe you're right. And by the way, what should we do about Buddy and Norm?"

"Go on the road trip until they divorce?"

"And then?"

"Then, lover boy, you are going to get your ass back out there and start making us some money because I'm going to blow your wad when we get to Vegas."

They both laughed and thought about it for a moment. Carol even reached across and touched his forearm. "I'll call your sisters in few days."

"Should I call Norm?"

"Nay, wait for him to call."

"How long should I wait?"

"Just until I can get all of our numbers changed."

"You see this: this is why Buddy screws up all the time. She's not loving and supporting like you."

"We are still not having another kid."

"Okay, but what about sex?"

"Oh, we can have sex anytime; you'll just have to wear a condom. I don't want you to infect me with your craziness."

"You know we are going to have to sit down with the kids and talk the whole weekend through."

"We will. When they are ready."

"How do you know they won't try bottling it up?"

"They are not programmed that way."

"You think I did the right thing with my father?"

"Johnnie, as long as I have known you, you have only done the right thing."

"Really?"

"Of course not. I was just saying that to be all loving and supportive. Except," she added after they had driven in silence for a while—silent except for the sound track of Grease. C.C. had made a point of leaving it in the player. "This time you did."

≈

"What can they say? What can anybody say?"

Gloria and Mary were sitting on the dock. They had just helped Jake into a canoe and pushed him gently away. He said it was something he had really wanted to do, and after much objection, Mary finally agreed—after she had insisted on a life jacket. Gloria noticed him slip it off just as he went behind the island, but Mary didn't. She had her head down

"What can who say?" she asked without raising it.

"What can who say about what?"

"You just said . . . oh, never mind."

Gloria didn't and rose slowly to fetch her tin box from under the loose board.

"Do you really think we should?" Mary asked and nodded her head towards where Jake had rounded the island. "What if he needs our help?"

"He is beyond our help now, Mary," Gloria responded slowly and solemnly. She packed her pipe and raised it to her lips. "All we can do now is to sit a while."

She lit it, and the flame of the match twinkled in the little teardrops in her eyes. She took a few hits and raised her head to the stars. "Have some," she offered without looking over.

"Perhaps I should wait until Jake is safely back."

Gloria lowered her head and turned. "Have some now. Jake won't be coming back."

Her hand was trembling, so Mary took the pipe before it fell. Her own hand began to tremble as she looked into Gloria's eyes. She could see all the way down to the old woman's torn heart. "Oh, Gloria, what have you done?"

"I have done what a mother has to do."

"But..."

"There wasn't anything else, Mary. It was his plan all along. He wanted to come and make as much peace as he could, and then he wanted to die here."

"But there had to have been some other way."

"He didn't think so and, God forgive me, I agreed with him."

"Oh, Gloria, why didn't you tell me?"

"What difference would it have made? Besides, that would have just made you an accomplice."

She meant it as a joke, but Mary was startled. "What about the police? What are they going to say?"

"What can they say? What can anybody say?"

"Well, there are laws..."

"Mary. Jake insisted on enjoying one last ride in the canoe. I let him. It would be ruled as misadventure at the most."

"You really thought this all through."

"Yes, I did. I really, really did, and in a little while I will call the authorities, but right now I need to sit here." She reached for the pipe again and Mary handed it back. She watched the old woman light another match and watched the cloud of smoke enshroud her like a spell.

She was staring at the island like she was trying to look through it.

"I sat right here with Harry when he died. It has a certain comforting symmetry."

"I wish I could have been there with you."

"Yes, that would have been nice, but you are here now, and I cannot think of anyone else I would want to share this with. It is a great privilege to share one's life with someone, and it is also a privilege to share death."

And as the sun settled lower, and the lake became burnished, the prow of the empty canoe drifted back into view. Dark and dreary against the color of the water, it turned like it knew the way and began to slowly drift towards them.

Neither woman spoke; everything had been said. They just sat together, each alone with their own thoughts and watched the canoe drift closer as the sun settled lower and lower.

Acknowledgments

My gratitude, as always, to Lou Aronica for his encouragement, support and guidance throughout.

And to Paula Pascu, whose enthusiasm is infectious.

About the Author

Peter Murphy was born in Killarney where he spent his first three years before his family had to move to Dublin. Growing up in the verdant braes of Templeogue, Peter was schooled by the De La Salle brothers in Churchtown where he played rugby for "The Wine and Gold." He also played football (soccer) in secret! After that, he graduated and studied the Humanities in Grogan's under the guidance of Scot's corner and the bar staff, Paddy, Tommy and Sean. Murphy financed his education by working summers on the buildings sites of London. He also tramped the roads of Europe playing music and living without a care in the world.

But his move to Canada changed all of that. He only came over for a while and ended up living there for more than thirty years. He took a day job and played music in the bars at night until the demands of family life intervened. Having raised his children and packed them off to university, Murphy answered the long-ignored internal voice and began to write. He has published five novels so far and has begun work on a new one. Nowadays, he lives in beautiful Lisbon with his wife Eduarda and their well-read dog, Baxter.

Reading Group Questions

1. Which character do you identify with most? Why?

2. Which is the most dysfunctional relationship in the story and why?

3. It seems as though every family has secrets. Why do you think this family felt it was so important to keep theirs? When are secrets acceptable, and when are they not?

4. Was Gloria right in insisting Jake visit his family?

5. How could Jake have handled his relationship with his older children more productively?

6. How does the environment (family cottage by the lake) affect the characters? Would you expect different responses had they been in another environment?

7. The author uses the motif of the summer's last weekend to symbolize the end of a "season" in a family. What will this family's "autumn" be like?

8. Which character do you think has changed most from the beginning of this novel to the end?

9. Which of the characters in the book do you think will benefit from this experience and which will not?

10. The author examines several marriages in this novel. Which of these do you think has been the most successful?

11. Do you think Jake was giving his family an opportunity to find closure, or do you think he was being self-indulgent?

12. Do you think C.C.'s place in the family has changed now that her parentage has been revealed?

13. Do you think Mary will be able to replace Gloria as the family matriarch?

14. Is the ending something you expected? If you could choose, how would you have ended the book?

A Conversation with the Author

Does writing energize or exhaust you?
In a nutshell, both. The actual process of sitting at the keyboard for long hours, trying to distill and sculpt from all that swirls around in my head can be physically and mentally demanding. But when it is flowing, I feel that I can write the whole book in one sitting – which I can't.

Do you try more to be original or to deliver to readers what they want?
This is a particular challenge for me, as I subscribe to the notion that a writer should write the books they would like to read, and my tastes in books, music, and art, tends to be closer to the fringe rather than the middle. However, for much of my life I played music for live audiences whose reactions and responses are immediate and obvious. By comparison, writing can be problematic in that the response comes after the book is printed. My hope is that with each book I learn a little more about my readers so I can coax them into reading about the things I think are worthy of their time and attention.

As a writer, what would you choose as your mascot/avatar/spirit animal?
Six years ago, my son went to the shelter and found a dog for me. Cute and beguiling, the little dog strolled into my life and established itself as my spirit guide.

Just today, while out for our morning walk in the glorious sunshine of Lisbon, a neighbor stopped to tell me that she wishes she could be more like my dog. In an odd mix of Portuguese and English, my neighbor explained that my dog was obviously a Zen master. My little Zen master has shown an uncanny knack for knowing when to disturb me – like when I, with chronic back issues, have been sitting too long. But then again, she might just be putting her own needs first. Life has a funny habit of looking after our real needs while we are busy doing other things.

What kind of research do you do, and how long do you spend researching before beginning a book?
As a child, I grew in an environment that was rich in story-telling. My mother, who I have now realized was wiser than most, forbade television, and we had to make do with the oral tradition. Much of what was said around me was the rich stuff of books.

My stories often start with those gems and, depending on the story, I can work from memory or spend months gathering "facts" and topical reactions.

This was a particularly large part of writing the trilogy, as it spanned a century of one family's history in very turbulent times while other characters were shadowed by the events of millennia. This meant collating chronologies and digging out newspaper articles and magazine commentaries and scanning reproductions of old manuscripts. At times I felt like a medieval scholar in some dusty old vault.

Do you view writing as a kind of spiritual practice?
Yes. As alluded to above, writing has had a profound impact on me as a person. And like many other writers, I am aware of the fickleness of muses and all the other pixies and gremlins that gather around a writer's shoulders when the midnight oil burns low.

I also think that life is a spiritual practice.

What's the most difficult thing about writing characters from the opposite sex?
The biggest challenge for me is, as a man, getting the sensitivities right in very sensitive times. We live in a world where words like cultural and gender appropriation flutter around our ears.

I recently read an impassioned rant from a gay activist calling on "straight" writers to stop writing "gay" characters. Likewise, I was set upon at a recent book club gathering by an angry feminist who accused me of creating "male fantasy" women. Such things, like much of what I hear and read these days, I briefly consider for insight and then discard and go on doing what I believe to be right.

I write about characters of the opposite sex (in my case women) with as much honesty, sympathy, and understanding as I can muster. To my mind, today's women have had some burdens lifted and some added. And while I support the correction of past wrongs, a less desirable aspect of any "ism" is that it creates a "them and us" mentality that causes us to be blind to our failings while focusing on "their" failings.

Women, like men, come in all shapes and sizes – physical, emotional, and mental. To write about them any other way would be pointless to me. I have had the great privilege of knowing a wide variety of women who are as great and as flawed as any writer could dream of.

Are your books biographical and how much of you, the author, can be found between the pages?
I do not write about myself, but I do write about things that happened all around me. Also, whether intentional or not, I believe that parts of the writer always seep in.
That said, a book full of characters that share my habits and views would be a very odd thing. Instead, I take stories that I know, twist and turn them for better readability, and fill them with all kinds of interesting people – many of whom do not share my own views or experiences.

I view my books as I do my adult children: part me, part their mother, and part of what has gone on before them and what has gone on around them.